# Erik's Tale

**The Phantom Saga**

Jessica Mason

Published by Murmuration Books, 2023.

This is a work of fiction. Similarities to real people, places, or events are entirely coincidental.

ERIK'S TALE

**First edition. October 17, 2023.**

ISBN: 979-8988421115

Written by Jessica Mason.

# Table of Contents

This book is for everyone who has felt different and alone.

To all the outcasts with hearts that could hold the empire of the world, you are loved.

# Author's Note

This little book happened by accident. When writing *Angel's Kiss*, Book Two of *The Phantom Saga* and there was so much more I wanted to include when it came to Erik's backstory, but I didn't have the space to accommodate it. This led to the idea of creating a separate document with all the backstory on its own and adding a few things, maybe to share somehow one day. In typical fashion for me, my ideas kept expanding and I found that Erik just had so much more to say. Soon it was clear that *Erik's Tale* was its own novella – the very one you are now reading. This book is meant to serve as a supplement to the larger story of *The Phantom Saga* and can be read at any point before, during, or after reading the main series.

In crafting Erik's narrative, I have tried as best I can to tell the story we know in a new way, but also in a way that is respectful and loving to the many places and cultures Erik encountered in his lifetime. I am incredibly grateful to the friends and sensitivity readers who gave their time and insight to make sure this book honors and empathizes with the diverse real cultures and places that shaped Erik's fictional life.

Finally, while this book is significantly less romantic and features less adult content than *The Phantom Saga*, there are still themes and content in this book that I wish to make readers aware of in case any of it may be triggering. This book contains violence and sexuality, as well as portrayals of child abuse, abuse of the disabled, and portrayals of individuals struggling with mental illness and substance abuse. Sexual assault occurs and is discussed, but is not portrayed in detail. For more detailed trigger warnings for this and the entire *Phantom Saga*, please consult my website: www.jessicamasonauthor.com[1].

Thank you for reading.

---

1.     http://www.jessicamasonauthor.com

# Prelude

*"Shall I tell you a story to pass the time?"*
*"A ghost story?"*
*"Or a wanderer's tale. Maybe a ballad of lost love?"*
*"I think you could manage all of them at once, if you tried. If you told your own story."*
*"You've asked me so many times to tell my tale. All of it. You know parts, of course. You know more than anyone of how I was born and grew and died to the world above to become a ghost. But you do not know it all, from beginning to end. I think it is high time to change that. Though it may not be easy to hear. Or to tell, come to think of it."*
*"I have great confidence in your skill."*
*"Then I hope I shall not disappoint you."*

I t is a hard thing, to put a life in order and make sense of it all.

Lives are like symphonies. They aren't built upon a single melody or created by one instrument. The theme changes and grows as time goes on, built up of a hundred sounds and a dozen motifs. We transition between keys and tempi as we grow, and the people we meet all add their harmony or dissonance. Some symphonies begin in thunder; some with one note. Some end far from where they began and some are unfinished. I would prefer to think of mine as the latter.

If I were to extend this already thin metaphor, what melody would we pick to begin? Something on a violin perhaps, or more accurately, a fiddle. Maybe a tin flute. I can hear them playing by the hearth. The

3

melody is one of longing and lost things, cool as the wind from the moors. Next to the fire was the warmest place in the little cottage with the thatched roof, or so my mother told me once.

Sometimes dreams of the past would intrude on her waking life and she'd think she was back there, close to the shore of the roiling sea, or near the ancient standing stones and green hills of Éire. Yes, an old Irish song would be a fitting theme on which to begin.

# 1. Rhapsody on an Irish Melody

*"This isn't your story."*
*"My story begins with hers."*

She was the fourth of six children, my mother, though two of her brothers didn't make it to their third year. Her father was a farmer with a home in the village of Coolaney, near Sligo. Conor Gilbride tilled the earth all week and took his family to sing in the church on Sunday, just as his father had done and his father before him. They did not own the land they worked – it belonged to the English lord of the manor, whom they never saw until it was time to pay their rent. Things were never easy there, but they found happiness where they could. Most of all in music, even if it was forbidden.

The English didn't let the Irish speak their native tongue nor sing the songs that lived in their blood, but they did it anyway. My mother heard those songs before she even drew her first breath, just like I did. And when she came into the world and grew up singing, she brought joy to her family and everyone around, that farmer's daughter with black hair who sang like a nightingale. She was blessed by Saint Brigid the bright they said, befitting her family name, little Sarah Gilbride.

Her voice delighted the whole village. My grandparents would take her to the Lughnasadh Fair, and she'd sing for the crowds from villages all around celebrating the first harvest. That was her favorite time of the year, when the green of the world had begun to fade to golden grains and hinted that autumn was near. She loved the bustle of the fair, the people. It reminded her of the wide world just out of reach for a little girl from a little town. But if her voice could take her to Sligo, maybe it could take her further. Maybe it could take her to a new life.

She grew up in the 1830s when everything in Ireland was starting to change. There were more people every year, but not more land or food. Life grew harder for the poor who worked the land, the fruit of their labor going to barons and viscounts a world away while their own families went hungry. Sarah dreamed of more and that dream filled her wild spirit. She would risk everything to find it, that 'more' always over the horizon.

I don't know if it's true, for so many of her stories came clouded with grief and regret, but my mother told me how once, on Beltane, when she was thirteen, she snuck off to the standing stones by the cemetery at Carrowmore and sang into the night, hoping that the Good Folk would take her away. She would have chosen to be a fairy's slave over a life wasted in a backward village at the edge of the world. Nothing happened – at least, not then. According to her, she was cursed after that. But I am getting ahead of myself, or rather, ahead of her.

People had started leaving Ireland before Sarah was born, but by the time she was fifteen, it seemed like families were heading west every month to start new lives. Her uncle joined them, then her oldest brother, taking the boat to America. This was before the great famine began in 1845 and drove all of Sarah's family from County Sligo. She left the year before that disaster, in 1844. She didn't want to go west though, rebel that she was. She thought her voice could take her somewhere better or to something greater. So she took the train to Dublin instead and then a boat to London.

She was quickly disappointed by the great metropolis. The only work for a sixteen-year-old Irish girl there was as a maid. There was no stage nor fame for her, only singing for the babes in the cradles rich women paid her to rock. Soon she began to miss the green hills and fresh air. Sneaking off to walk in the sooty fog by the Thames was nothing like walking by the sea on a gray day at home. But Sarah did not give up easily. She was smart and hardworking, and impressed her employers, earning herself better jobs and positions.

Eventually, she found herself in a fine house where she waited on the fine noblewomen, including a very impressive guest: a baroness from France. She was so fascinated by young Sarah that she hired her on the spot and took her home across the Channel to the family's fine château, near Rouen. Sarah hoped she could save enough working there to go to Paris, the city of her dreams. She believed no one in Paris would care if she was Irish like they had in London. *There* she would have a chance at the elusive 'more' she had always dreamed of. But she would never get that far.

She was happy at the château in the picturesque village of Yville-sur-Seine, for a few weeks at least, as winter faded. She loved spring in the gardens and all the flowers she had never seen before. She caught the eye of a stonemason who was building a new chapel on the grounds. He caught her singing out the Baroness's window one day and tipped his hat. When he learned how much she loved the flowers, he brought her a bouquet of the first cherry blossoms of the year. Everything was hopeful and good, until the spring returned in earnest, and with it, the son of the old Baron and Baroness, home after a journey abroad.

His name was Alfred, and he quickly took a liking to the pretty new Irish maid. Sarah was smart though, and saw that he was a cad at the least and dangerous at the most. When he pursued her, she demurred. She said no to him many times, but after a week, he decided to take what he wanted and rape her. She was just the young maid, she could barely speak French! She wasn't a *person*. She was a thing to be exploited and enjoyed.

I don't like to think about how I was conceived. No child born of such violence does, I'm sure. Thankfully, my mother never told me in any detail what happened, but for years after she had nightmares, and I heard her cries in the night. She told him to stop, to leave her alone, that she'd tell everyone what he'd done. He didn't care. I think that monster enjoyed it more that way.

My mother never stopped fighting him. For months Alfred abused her, but she couldn't get away. She couldn't tell anyone. She couldn't go home in shame. She barely spoke the language, and who would believe her anyway? It was only when the Baroness realized her new maid had somehow gotten with child, that Sarah was forced to confess.

The Baroness – my grandmother – intervened too late, exiling her son to Paris. My mother thought she was free, finally. There was the problem of the child in her belly, but that could be dealt with, even if it damned her soul further. She didn't care anymore. Before Alfred, Sarah had been a good Catholic girl; she'd agreed to come to France because the people there shared her faith. But the saints were different in that new land, even if the Blessed Virgin was still the same. And all of them – saints, Virgin, Father, Son, and Holy Spirit – they had abandoned her to be raped and ruined. So she decided to defy them and save herself.

She went to a woman in the village to get rid of the child that the monster had put in her. Sarah had grown up among the midwives and the herbalists and she knew them and their art well. But just like her saints, this cunning woman failed her as well. Whatever that woman gave my mother to expel the child growing in her womb didn't work. The evil inside her was too strong and the child growing in her became something terrible and deformed.

At least, that was the tale she would tell me; as if I was to blame for what I became. Because I refused to die and free her, we were both condemned.

When it was clear she had failed to end the pregnancy, my mother wanted to try again or kill herself. She told me that many times too. But the Baroness stopped her, even over the protests of her husband, who found out about the whole ordeal when my mother was brought inside the château screaming after she was found at the edge of the roof. They kept her under lock and key after that and resolved to keep her and their grandchild close. My grandmother was the only blood relation who wanted me alive – I was her first grandchild after all. She did what was needed to ensure my survival.

I don't know what kind of threats or deals were made, but by the end of the summer, my mother was married off to the stonemason who had wooed her with posies in the spring. She discovered before the wedding that his flowers had been a lie, brought only in the hopes he could fuck her. In truth, he was a useless lout named Carl who saw the arrangement as an easy way to stay on the payroll. He didn't mind that my mother was pregnant with a bastard so long as the Baroness gave him his money. He thought he'd be able to take his rights as a husband, but my mother would have none of that.

Carl and Sarah were married in the little chapel in the village, before men and God, and both the men and God knew it was a farce. The Baroness sent them across the Seine, to a cottage on a plot of land that Carl was supposed to tend. The Baroness made sure my mother was watched and the household was taken care of by hiring a half-blind maid from Finland to keep us alive – Aneka. It was a humble home, but it was livable and maybe someone else could have been happy there.

Perhaps the entire story could have been different if it hadn't been for my face.

I was born in the dark of winter, earlier than expected. They thought I was dead at first. I'm told the midwife screamed when I moved and began to cry. I looked like a corpse when I took my first breath and yet, I refused to die. Someone called for a priest, either to perform an exorcism or deliver a baptism for the sickly, monstrous thing that had fought its way into the world. My mother refused to let him in; said she didn't care for my soul. She didn't want to see me, didn't want me to live. But finally, she looked.

That was what finally broke her; to see that the child her tormentor had left her with was a different kind of monster. She went mad when she saw me and tried to throw me against the wall, according to Carl. And still, I would not die. Aneka forced her to nurse me, but my mother only did it after making a mask out of an old kerchief, so she could look at me without the urge to dash my head against the floor or scream.

I only know stories about my first months of life. Everyone kept waiting for me to die, but I didn't. I kept breathing. Carl left as soon as the snow melted, Aneka kept everyone fed. Feeding the animals and the useless humans were no different for her. She reported to the Baroness, so she wasn't afraid of slapping my mother out of her stupors to make her eat or nurse me or drugging her tea when she started to scream back at me when I cried.

The only thing that made me stop crying, I know, was when my mother sang. She didn't sing for me though; she sang for herself. She'd sing old songs of her homeland and transport herself far away from the miserable prison her life had become. My earliest memory is sneaking into her room and listening to those songs, and Aneka shooing me away like I was a dog when she found me.

Or more accurately a cat. Aneka was the one who named all the animals, all names from her homeland, so that our farmstead sounded like a Viking mead hall. Olaf. Lars. Sven. Harald. Erik. She noticed how I'd perk up when she called Erik the cat, who I played with when he'd let me. So she called me Erik too. My mother didn't use the name until later, when she accepted that somehow, I had survived into another year. No matter what I was called, I was still a monster, just like my father.

"Erik. As good a name as any for a curse." I remember those words from before I could understand what they meant.

If I was her curse, she was mine in those early years. She had been broken by the cruelty of the world before I was born, this grotesque thing she had never asked for, and now she was barely eighteen, married to a man she hated, stuck with a child she never wanted, destroyed and abused. She was shattered by the time I started to reason and perceive the world. Out of some instinct, I wanted to be near her, longed for her to comfort me. Rarely did she give me anything but pain.

I've known since I was old enough to know anything, that I was ugly. I didn't need mirrors to see it because everyone around me was my mirror. I saw their revulsion when I took off my mask, I heard their words and insults, and I felt the sting of their beatings. Only an ugly, terrible thing would deserve that. One day, when I had misbehaved in some way, my mother did put me in front of a mirror to punish me and I saw at last the monster I was. How I screamed at the sight.

As I grew older, my mother grew more mad and more broken. One day, she would be wild and violent; the next week, she would not leave her bed. She called me a changeling, sometimes, when her mind was afire. She would say the fairies had taken her real son and replaced him with the withered corpse of one of their own. She'd scream at me and shake me, demanding I reveal my true nature. She hated my face with such a passion that she'd lose her mind when I took off the mask.

I was four, old enough to form memories, when I refused to put it on. It was so uncomfortable in the summer! I knew I was ugly, awful, but surely it didn't matter if no one saw, if I could just wander our overgrown fields and feel the sun on my cheeks and the wind on my skin. Aneka wasn't there to hold her off when she snapped and turned into the stuff of my nightmares. For years after that, I'd hear her screams as she chased me down, terror and guilt filling my heart until I thought it would explode.

She said if I wanted to take the mask off, she'd take off my face. I was used to her clawing and striking me, but that day, she found a knife. In her madness, she tried to relieve me of my face and only made my ugliness worse. I knew the pain of a beating, I knew fear and love, but that day was the first one I truly knew the hopeless terror that would seize me anys time she raised her voice or hand after that. It scarred me far deeper than my flesh.

Aneka stopped her halfway through and beat her back into her bed. She didn't come out of her room for a week after, and I was glad of it. Aneka refused to intervene and get her errant mistress out. It was Carl who forced her back to life. He came home from another month of spending the Baroness' money on wine and bad bets to find his so-called wife in a soiled bed, babbling about the fair folk in a language he didn't know.

I remember how he forced her to wash and how she screamed the whole time, then wept. And then she called my name for help. I should have hated her. I was so afraid but she was still Mama. Somehow, I knew to call her that and I didn't want her to cry anymore. I chased Carl away and crept up to where she was cowering in a corner. I sang her the song she'd hum to herself when she was at her worst.

"*There were three ravens sitting on a tree, with a down, a down, hey down, hey down. They were as black as black could be...*"

And she came back. It was strange: I was the one that drove her mad, and yet, I was the only one who could calm her when she was at her worst and it was music that did it. Her voice had always entranced and soothed me, so when I realized I could sing too, I thought I could finally make her love me. Children believe such foolish things, I know.

I could make her calm, for a time when she fell into despair or mania. At night I'd sing to myself too. I'd sing myself to sleep in the dark, old Irish songs I learned from her that made me dream of a distant land I'd never seen. I loved them, because, for all her madness and cruelty, I loved the woman who gave me life, because she was all I knew.

I hated Carl though. I blamed him for all my pains and ills, and my mother didn't stop me. Over the years, he began to resent the bargain he'd made. It was fine for him to travel about and gamble or drink his life away, but he wanted a home to come back to as much as anyone else, I guess, and he resented that he didn't have it. Instead, he had a madwoman and a petit monster who had started talking back when given orders.

He tried, more than once, to take his rights as a husband and my mother threatened to cut off his manhood. Once, he tried to beat her, and I came to her defense. I threw off my mask to scare him away and it worked. My mother struck me for daring to show my face and remind her. But that night she sang to me and I sang back. She just made sure she couldn't see me when she did.

When she was not in a fit of depression or screaming and ranting in madness, my mother could be almost human. She taught me to speak and then to write and read out of pure defiance. It had been a rebellion on her father's part to teach a girl to read, not only English but Irish too. And so she rebelled when Carl said teaching me anything was as useless as teaching a pig to dance. After that, he found a pig in his bed, and my mother started lessons.

They were hard, and she was a cruel teacher, but I learned everything fast. Her spite was the reason that I learned anything, but it was my fear and a naïve desire to impress and please her that made me the most eager and quick of students.

Another rebellion came one day my mother spent all of our stipend on a little piano, before Carl could take it. He beat us both for it, but the piano stayed, and I taught myself to play. It wasn't my first instrument; I'd already learned to make melodies on a tin flute my mother had brought from Ireland. Carl hated it when we played, so we played louder to annoy him.

It was to spite Carl as well that she started drinking his wine before he could get to it. And soon the only love they shared was for drowning their misery in alcohol. It terrified me, at first, when they were both drunk. I didn't know if they would fight or fall over and never wake up.

But soon I learned that drunkenness led to dreamless, deep sleep, and that in turn meant I could slip out of the house to freedom.

I loved to wander the woods and fields at night. I made friends with the stars and moon, learned secret paths from animals. In the day I wasn't allowed past our gate or into the village, but at night, I could go anywhere. And there were no people in the quiet of the night to hurt me or tell me how ugly and wrong I was. Maybe the rest of the world was like that. I wanted to be free, to see the wide world, just as my mother had when she was small. My favorite place to go was the church.

I'd trace the names and words on the gravestones and pretend to talk to the ghosts. Or perhaps I did talk to them, who can say? The dead were kinder than the living, that was for sure. But the real reason I came was for the music. I didn't entirely understand the church. I knew it was where people went to find God, and I knew God had power and magic, and was worthy of being adored.

I heard the music of the organ and the choir, and I recalled how my voice could soothe my mother and save me, and I believed with all my small heart that music *was* God. It was so beautiful, and even a monster such as I could share in it. It was magic and it was always there for me when I found myself in despair.

The only person who could inspire any sort of respect among a family that hated each other so much was the woman who kept us together, the Baroness. She would visit every other month or so and always wanted to see me, or at least know I was alive. I didn't understand her interest in me, since I thought Carl was my father until I could speak. I had the audacity to call him "Papa" instead of "Sir" one day and I can still hear the hate in his voice when he corrected me.

"I'm not your father, you little bastard. It was the baron's son who stuck you in your mother's belly and left you to rot." As well as I can remember those words, I can recall how scared they made me feel. I didn't want Carl as a father, but some awful stranger sounded worse. I had the right instinct.

I asked my mother later that night when she was deep in her cups. I remember she was singing to herself, with the fire warming her face, an old song of Ireland. I sang along and she closed her eyes and smiled for just a moment. And I asked: if Carl was not my father, who was?

I braced myself for her to strike me. But she just laughed. "Your father is a monster, just like you." I'll never forget those words either.

I learned the story in pieces. My mother and Carl wielded the truth of my lineage and conception like knives to strike at me when I misbehaved and a beating wouldn't be punishment enough. I dreamed about who my father might be. In my heart, he was someone who cared for beauty and sound the way I did. But I knew I did not have his voice. I don't think my mother would have let me live if I had reminded her too much of him.

It was a year before I asked the Baroness if she was really my grandmother. She looked sad when she nodded. I asked her to take me away, and just like everyone, she laughed. But her laugh was kind. We were walking in the garden, my mask firmly in place as it always had to be around her and we could hear my mother and Carl screaming about money back in the house. I told her that surely life with her would be better. Was she afraid of me? Carl hurt Mama and she hurt me. My father had hurt my mother. Did my grandmother not want to save me because she was afraid that *I* would hurt people too? She didn't laugh at that.

"There are good men in the world. I hope you know that," she told me. Her husband was good, she said. They had married for love, and he had promised to love her to the stars and beyond. She showed me the words on her gold ring that I liked to play with. They had thought their love would beget a child that was good and kind, but they had been wrong. I cried at that, but she told me not to weep. Maybe there was hope: if a child born of love could sow nothing but hate, perhaps a child begotten by hate could believe in love. It was a foolish dream, but I held onto it for a while before I learned how cruel the world truly was.

What more can I say of my childhood in my mother's care? The Baroness wanted me to have tutors, I recall. She saw how I could read and spell as well as a boy twice my age. She knew I had a talent for music too, but my mother refused. She didn't want anyone near me or in our house. Sometimes she was proud, it seemed, when I showed how quick my mind was or how easily I could pick up a tune. But then a shadow would fall over her, and she'd say not to dream. Music and wits didn't save her, and she was normal, they wouldn't save me.

It takes us a while, when we're older, to realize the ways our parents were wrong. She was wrong about that. Music had already saved me. It saved me all the time, from her and from the close, terrible walls of that little cottage I only escaped at night.

The old Baron died the spring after I turned eight. It was a wet, cold day when we heard the news, and I remember how my mother laughed. Her laugh had been gentle once, but as she grew older and the madness took her, it had grown into something cruel and empty. She said something about how the old man could hold a place for his son in Hell. I wanted to go to the funeral, even though I had never met the man, and she slapped me for suggesting it. I looked for him in the graveyard by the church, but he wasn't buried there. He was interred in the family crypt at the château's chapel.

I expected the Baroness to come and visit after, veiled in black and heartbroken. But she didn't. Something was wrong. Then, the money stopped. Carl was back from gambling away the last payment by then and he didn't like that. So he decided it was a good idea to barge up to the château and demand the new Baron support his bastard. My mother tried to stop him. I wish she had succeeded.

Carl didn't come back by nightfall, but one of the Baron's valets did. A man in a fancy livery out of another century. He demanded we present ourselves to the Baron, and he wouldn't leave until we went with him. I was afraid, not for Carl or myself, but for my mother. In all my life of watching her fight her demons, I had always seen her raging and screaming against them. I'd never seen her cower or shake in fear, but when we were summoned to see the man who had defiled her to make me, she look truly scared. And that terrified me.

It was my first time meeting my father. I'd always wanted to see the monster my mother blamed for my existence. I wanted to know if one could perceive the evil in him, like people could in me. But when we walked into his grand house and he met us in his fancy room full of porcelain and gold and fresh flowers, the man who met us was as handsome as the home he now owned. I had my mother's dark hair, he had hair so blonde it was almost white. His eyes were cold, blue as ice on a frozen winter day. My eyes were gold, or so I had been told. I'd never seen them. The monster in the mirror always closed his eyes before I could look too long.

We weren't entirely dissimilar, however. He was tall and long, the way I was starting to look, and I could tell he frightened people too. I looked for the white hair of the dowager Baroness, but she wasn't home. I'd find out later that Carl was in the cellar, drunk and beaten. We were alone with the monster, and for the first time in my life, my mother held onto my hand for comfort so tight it hurt.

"It's good to see you again, sweet Sarah," he said when we came in. He didn't look at me, only the plaything he had been told was sent away. "To think you've been here all along. Right under my nose. And now you send that lout begging for our bastard's sake."

My mother stood straight at that. "Let him beg. I need nothing from you. I want nothing from you. I'd leave this hell in an instant if I could." It hurt to hear her call our life hell, but I knew it wasn't a lie.

"If you could?" he asked back and finally looked at me. "Is it this child that chains you here? Let me see him. Let me see my son."

She ripped off my mask before I could run or protest. I remember the disgust on that handsome face when he saw me. There had been a small part of me that had hoped that he – my father, even if he was a monster – would look at me with love. But there was only revulsion and it confirmed how she had taught me to hate that man. "A face to match his father's soul," my mother said. "Pay us and let us go. Then you'll never hear from us again."

"No." It was such a simple answer, but my mother started to scream in the face of his callousness. Then everything happened so fast. He came at us and tossed my mother aside like she was nothing, then he grabbed me and threw me in a wardrobe of all things. I guess anything with a lock would have sufficed.

I screamed; a terror like I had never known overtaking me. I was so afraid. She was the strong one, the one who started my pain and stopped it and she was in the clutches of the man I had been told all my life was the worst person in the world. I screamed for someone to help, I screamed for my mother. I pounded against the door and felt the latch start to give, but not soon enough. I can still remember the dark. The smell of his fresh linens and shoe polish. And I remember the way my mother wailed in terror. Even as a child, I knew what he was going to do. I knew I had to stop it. I had to protect her, but I was small and foolish and so scared.

She had sworn, my mother, she had *sworn* to never let a man violate her again. Especially him. So she fought, and so did I. The door gave out at last, and I saw them: my father pushing her against the bed, perhaps the same bed he had sired me in. Her clothes were torn and her eyes were wild. My father looked at me and froze. Maybe it was my face, maybe it was that I had broken free. But that brief moment of distraction gave my mother the seconds she needed to get away.

She didn't run to the hall or the door. She knew he would catch her. She ran to the window instead, shattering the glass as she threw herself against it. It was quiet for the longest moment imaginable before I heard her hit the ground. And then someone else screamed below.

I ran down to her. Maybe she had survived it. She looked like she was asleep when I found her. So peaceful. More peaceful than I had ever seen her. I had always been able to wake her up. To bring her back. So I sang to her in the dark, as people gathered around us. My first requiem.

My world lay dead and broken on the cold ground. The woman who had given me a life full of pain yet kept me nourished with crumbs of hope, was gone. Everything I knew was gone, and I thought my own life would end right there. But it didn't. I kept going. I kept breathing.

I don't remember much after that. My father was there, unphased by his crime. Someone grabbed me when I tried to attack him. *He* killed her, as sure as shooting her. Just like I had, by being born. If I had already killed her, why couldn't I kill him? But I was small; a wild, broken child.

"Get that thing out of my sight," my father said before I was hauled away. I cried and screamed that night so much I couldn't speak the next day. It felt right, to be as silent as she was in the grave.

I hope that when she jumped, she felt like she was going to freedom at last.

# 2. Waltz à la Vienne

*"He should have been held accountable."*
*"I was soon to learn that men like him are rarely held to account by any laws of men. It is for people like us to take fate into our own hands."*

I don't remember much about the days after my mother died. The Baroness took over, exiling her horrid son once again. Years later, I would learn that he was shipped off to be married, as if that would do anything but damn some other poor woman.

They buried my mother on the grounds, by the chapel Carl helped build. I wanted to see her gravestone or sing her a song, like the people did in the church, but I wasn't allowed. My grandmother wouldn't look at me, not because of my face or my mask, but I think because she knew she could have stopped this if she had just let my mother go years before. She wouldn't make the same mistake again. She gave Carl a thousand francs and told him to disappear forever with me.

He dragged me to Le Havre, and to my young eyes that had barely seen the village where I grew up, the port town seemed the grandest, biggest city in the world. It was so crowded and loud. All I wanted to do was hide away from the thunder of all the carriages and the shouts of the workers on the docks. There were *people* everywhere and they all looked at me, the strange little boy in the mask. I didn't like it and neither did Carl. He made me wear a hood and smacked me if I stared at anything too long. I remember seeing the ocean for the first time. It was so big and wild and it made me feel so small. No matter how many times he struck me, I never stopped looking at it that first day.

We crossed the Channel to Brighton, where it was equally as packed and deafening, only this time, the people spoke a language I'd only heard from my mother. I liked listening to the novel words as we traveled to London. Carl's English was terrible, so he made me translate half the time, and the people we met were more than suspicious of a Frenchman with a young boy in a mask as his translator. I spent most of my time scared, confused, and hungry. The only consolation I had was to sing to myself, but Carl caught me and boxed my ears for making noise that kept him awake.

When we got to London, we took rooms in the worst part of the city. It was so dark there all the time, the skies gray with fog and smoke from factories and for the first time, my heart ached for home, awful as it had been. Carl threatened to sell me to one of those factories many times but stopped because (he claimed) they wouldn't give him a fair price or take a monster.

I wouldn't see him for days. He drank and gambled away the Baroness's money in a few weeks, but I liked it better when he was gone. Then I could sing and look out the windows, hoping to see a sliver of blue sky. I believed he intended for us to go to Dublin to find someone from my mother's family to leave me with if any of them were left that hadn't gone to America after the famine. But he found a much more lucrative and convenient prospect while he was exploring and saw advertisements for a very particular type of show. Or maybe it was better termed an exhibit. It caught his attention and sealed my fate.

One fateful night two weeks into our stay, he returned to the room and fed me something that tasted wrong. I fell asleep and woke up in a cage in a train car. Without my mask.

I had spent much of my life being afraid. Afraid of my mother, of Aneka, of Carl. But I had always had a place to hide and the consistency of home to protect me. There had been music, and as a child, I had foolishly believed in the fairy tale of a better day on the horizon. All of that was gone when I woke up in that stinking box, the roar of the train tracks shaking my small body. I had never been more frightened or confused.

But I wasn't alone.

When I screamed for help, a voice called out to comfort me, and then a figure came around where I could see. The woman who told me to stop crying and calm down had the blackest skin I'd ever seen. She spoke English with a strange accent I didn't know when she told me not to be afraid. I still was. She said if I was good, no one would hurt me. She seemed so kind and I stopped crying. I don't think she meant to lie – about no one hurting me.

Her name was Rose, and she informed me that she, like myself now, was the property of Klaus Steiner, an impresario. I protested: people weren't allowed to own people. I didn't know much, but I knew that, thanks to rants from my mother about the English, and even Carl's few bouts of sense. Rose laughed at that. It was sad and resigned. She said that might be true where I was from, but in her world – in the world where I had now found myself – there was no freedom. Not for people like us. I didn't understand what that meant. Like us?

"*Freaks.*"

It is an English word: freak. We don't have quite the same word in French. Something that encompasses the odd and the bizarre; the people who are too different to ever fit in the normal world. The closest word we have is *monstre*. Rose helped me to understand as well as she could. A boy like me with a face like death was a freak and Steiner collected that sort of person.

Steiner had been on tour with Rose and a few other human peculiarities in London when he had bought me from Carl. We were on our way to his home now, Vienna, where he kept his museum of living *oddities*. His human zoo of freaks.

He wasn't an innovator, Steiner. He'd learned his craft from successful Americans in New York. He would talk enviously about a man there who had passed off a blind slave as George Washington's nursemaid. He was the only charlatan or showman of his kind in Vienna, however. That city sounded so far away to me. Rose told me we were already back on the continent. It wouldn't be long before I was in my new home. Maybe then, Steiner would let me out.

The journey was long and awful. I didn't meet Steiner himself until I'd spent two days suffering in my little cage, something I think was meant for hunting dogs or livestock. He brought something that passed for a meal and told me to not even think about refusing it or I'd be in for a beating. I looked through his legs at Rose, at the way she pled with her dark eyes for me to do as I was told. I reached through the bars, took the bowl of slop he had offered, and threw it on Steiners shiny shoes. I said I wanted to go home, even though I had none.

I wasn't afraid of the pain that came in return for my defiance, though the way Steiner whipped my back raw with his belt was new. I knew how to take a beating. I could retreat into my mind and go numb. Rose screamed for him to stop until he struck her too and that only increased my resolve. I didn't eat a scrap of food that night, only the next day when Rose snuck me some of hers. By the time we reached Vienna, I was hungry and hurting, but I wasn't broken yet. My mother's stubborn defiance lived on in me.

Steiner owned an establishment in that great city, close to the new *Ringstrasse*, the great avenue being built to replace the old city walls that had stood for centuries. It was a grand theater from the outside, but everything behind the curtains was rotten and terrible. It had a smell though, of dust and old wood and wax that I've come to know every theater has. Maybe it was haunted too, I'm not sure. We were all kept there, his menagerie of mis-made flesh, some with better quarters than others. I was sent into a room in the cellars with my cage and no other bed. I'd have to earn comfort with obedience.

I refused.

I refused to speak or eat. I fought like a demon when Steiner first came to pull me out to be exhibited. The whipping I got for wasting his money didn't break me, nor did the one after that. I was adamant I would escape. I'd find my way home or somewhere better. I was eight, so you must forgive my delusions and my defiance. But I didn't want to let that man win.

I should have. I should have crumbled before he sent me to the real hell below the theater. It was built as a carnival maze, but it didn't make any money, so Steiner repurposed all those mirrors into a new sort of prison for freaks. He'd turned the mirrors on themselves so they reflected like a kaleidoscope.

He was a smart man, Steiner. He knew how to control and break his animals. He knew the worst thing he could do to a little monster like me was show me the thing that scared me most: myself. He shut me in that little room with a lamp and nothing but infinite copies of my own dead face to look at. It was a torture chamber.

And I finally screamed. I screamed for what felt like hours and promised to be good. I shut my eyes, but the monster was there in my mind, dead and awful and cursed, the scars my mother had given me making my ugliness all the worse. I cried and begged. I thought I'd die there.

Rose was the one to let me out of the torture chamber. She didn't hold me or wipe my tears. She offered me stale bread and a blanket and petted me like the pathetic, wild creature I was before she left. I wasn't allowed out of the cellar. I stayed there, utterly alone and wishing I could just die and be done with it.

And then I heard it: a sound like something straight from heaven. Music. It was slow and steady. Only violins, and another sound, melancholy and small, but so beautiful. A clarinet. In a melody that rose above everything, like the voice of God once again coming from the dark. I had found myself below the concert hall next to our theater.

From above me like the voice of an angel, music like I had never heard came to save me.

I'd learn later that the author of this magic was Mozart. It was the Clarinet Concerto in A, the Adagio. It was perfect. It was through that music that I remembered how to hope, and I knew then I could live. I had to stay so I could be close to these sounds and discover how to be part of them, to make them even.

I learned later that I was in Mozart's city, and that became a consolation to me as well. Mozart wasn't born in Vienna; he had come as a child to the city that valued music as highly as gold. I'd sneak into the cellars and under the concert hall any time I could. I listened to the precise clockwork of Bach, and the refined, aloof melodies of Händel that could somehow still stir the very soul. I smiled at the warmth of Haydn, and I shivered at the fury of Beethoven. It was the music that kept me there and kept me alive.

I kept the memory of Mozart playing in my mind when Steiner finally put me on stage. I was kept behind a screen at first, my ankles chained so I couldn't run when the curtain fell away at Steiner's command to reveal me to the waiting crowd. The first time I was exhibited, I tried to keep my eyes closed, to keep hearing those perfect sounds in my head. They could drown out the gasps, the words of shock in a tongue I didn't know.

But Steiner's whip cracked with a command to open my eyes, and I obeyed. The corpse the crowd saw before them opened its eyes. They saw a dead boy come alive and they screamed. And I saw the horror in all their living, normal faces.

*"Schauen Sie mal! Der Lebendige Tod!"* Steiner cried. *Feast your eyes on The Living Death!* I was back in the torture chamber, reflected a hundred times in all those eyes, and all the pain came right back. He beat me that night for weeping when I looked back at my horrified audience, but he always kept the wounds he left where no onlooker would see.

Rose told me it would get easier. I trusted her. But when I finally met them, I saw the same despair in the eyes of my fellow freaks as I felt up on that stage. It did get easier, that was true, but being displayed was never without pain or degradation. It was never easy in and of itself. Not for any of us.

Steiner had a dozen or so people in various forms of bondage to him. Some he bought and some he paid. None he treated like humans. There was a man, Gus, with a third arm; a withered thing on his side that he could barely move. Phineas was covered in tattoos from head to toe. Ezra was covered in hair like a dog. He escaped after a year. I envied him. There was Gutrune, an acrobat who moved like she had no bones, and an old sailor called Bill missing an arm and a leg who claimed he had lost them to a kraken. He was paid in drink and snored through his shows when he wasn't ranting.

Rose was exhibited as a "Hottentot Aphrodite" or a "Congo queen." She was neither. She'd been born on a plantation in America and sold as a child, and her curves and dark skin saw her eventually make her way into Steiner's hands. Slavery had been illegal in Austria for a while, but that didn't matter to Steiner, and he threatened all the time to send Rose back to where he had found her, where he claimed life was even worse. In his care at least she was a star, he claimed, a Nubian queen that the people could ogle and admire. Rose was too smart to laugh at that and agreed, but when he was gone, she'd call him a fool for speaking of a life he didn't know.

Rose was the only reason I lived through those first few months. She was that rare sort of person who meets the worst of the world with kindness and hope. She hated her place in the world, but she did her best in it and tried to help me do the same. I never listened.

It took me a while to not be afraid she'd beat me because I simply expected any adult to hurt me or treat me like a monster. She never did.

She fed me, spoke to me in English, and taught me my first words of German, words she'd learned in secret. Steiner didn't want us to speak the local language, you see; it made us more unlikely to escape if we couldn't ask for help. We defied him in that. He could keep our bodies trapped, but not our minds, and many of us learned enough. Those who could.

Sebastian was another deformed boy, but he was different from me. He looked like a figure of clay the gods had twisted in the womb; human, but distorted. He couldn't speak and moved strangely, but he was kind and gentle. He'd only listen to his sister, Constance. She took care of him and did her own act throwing knives and axes, but she couldn't always protect him from Steiner, who treated him like a dog.

When Sebastian misbehaved, he'd be sent to the torture chamber in the cellar just like me, until Constance intervened. She'd go into Steiner's private offices and return with the keys. She stole them or went to his bed. It varied. But she did what she had to in order to protect her brother as well as she could. I had no one like that to protect me. Rose didn't want me to die, because she had a kind heart and an affection for lost creatures. But she wasn't family. She wasn't a way out.

All I had to give me real hope was music. Rose may have been the person who kept me alive, but music was the reason I wanted to stay that way.

Within a few months, I learned how to slip from the cellar of our theater into the bowels of the concert hall next door and I began to haunt the place in the dark recesses of the night. I took pieces of music – anything I could find – and tried to learn it. I borrowed instruments as well, and my juvenile experiments had varying degrees of success. The clarinet and flute were easier to navigate than the tuba. I'd always return them after I was done, long before dawn. Years later I heard a rumor that the theater next door was haunted. People heard strange music playing there at the oddest times of night...

It was nearly a year before I realized that I could do more than slip into the other theater. I could flee my prison into the night just as I had done back home. But exploring a great city like Vienna in the dark was far different than the woods and churchyards of rural France. I started slowly, always making it back before dawn, when Steiner would check on his stock.

First, I went to the *Stephansplatz* and the great cathedral with spires that surely were tall enough to scratch the moon. I had never seen such a building, a gothic palace for a dangerous and distant god. But there were real palaces just steps away, in the *Hofburg*, where the Emperor and his new bride lived. People said she was the most beautiful woman in Europe, but the one time I caught a glimpse of her walking from the palace into a carriage, her incredible, long hair flowing behind her like a river of silk, she looked like the saddest.

By my tenth year, I knew the city like the back of my hand. The farthest I went from the theater was to the great *Zentralfriedhof*, the only cemetery in Vienna. It was so big wild animals made their homes there, in the forgotten corners. Somewhere in that maze, I learned, Mozart had been thrown into a pauper's grave, so I could not pay my respects. But Beethoven was there, his great headstone like an idol I could kneel before to pay my respects and ask a blessing. It made me feel less lonely, those nights when I walked among the headstones and ghosts, deer walking silently in the shadows beside me.

The whole city was mine at night. I traipsed through narrow streets in the moonlight, in search of music like it was gold. Even at night, there were musicians on the streets or playing in concert halls or salons. The churches great and small echoed with masses and requiems. No city I have visited since, even Paris, had music in its very blood the way Vienna did. I think that was why I never ran, not just the fear of what Steiner would do to the others if one of us escaped, but because Vienna welcomed me, aloof and alien as she was, her music became my home.

And I stayed because of that, not just because I had come to care for my fellow curiosities.

We were not a family, all of us ensnared by Steiner, by his design. He tried not to let us form too many bonds, to keep us obedient and dependent, but we still found ways to band together. We respected one another. We understood the burdens we bore as ones who would always be marked as others, never welcomed by the kind of people who paid to gawk at us. And so, I was taken in by my compatriots. I was the youngest one there by far, but I was clever and curious. Slowly, each of the freaks found something to teach me when I couldn't teach myself.

I learned how to hold my own in a fight from Gus, and how to pick locks and escape ropes or chains from Ezra. Rose and I spoke in English and practiced our reading and writing together, and I taught her French in exchange for more lessons in German. Bill told me stories of the places he had visited, Phineas taught me to play cards – and then how to cheat at them. Constance smuggled me books and taught me to throw knives because Sebastian liked it when I sang.

There were others to learn from, not just other freaks. Steiner always wanted variety in his establishment and had no qualms about who he hired. So very often he would bring in groups of Roma to round out the lineup and work the crowd. The Roma seemed to me the very altar of the mystic. They spoke in secret words. Even though the crowds that came through Steiner's theater looked at them as vagrants or dangerous, they still flocked to them to have their fortunes told or to see them perform magic and illusion, or dance. I was fascinated by them.

Once, when I was small back in France, I'd snuck off to the woods and heard a Romani fiddler playing by a fire, and the music had been like the fire itself. When I was finally brave enough and allowed to speak to the Roma who came to the theater, I sought out a fiddler among them and begged him to teach me.

His name was Ivo. It took a few days of my pestering for him to say yes, but eventually, he took pity on the strange boy in the canvas mask (Steiner had finally started to let me wear one). I took to it instantly, and I still remember the awe in my teacher's eyes when I perfectly replicated an air I had only heard once.

A few days later, when he heard me, Steiner wondered aloud if I had made a deal with the devil to play so well so easily. I didn't deny it. Then I saw a fear in my teacher's eyes. It was a different kind of fear than the terror in the eyes of an audience. There was respect behind it. That was when I learned again how music could be my ally, how it could serve as another mask between me and the gawking crowds that came to see my hideous face. And so could magic.

Other performers came through the theater, with different bands of Roma or on their own. As I grew, I learned from all of them. I learned sleight of hand, I learned to speak without moving my lips. And each day I practiced on any instrument I could find or sang. Because all of it had the power to change what I was. Not the reflection in the mirrors of the torture chamber where I was still sent when I learned too much too fast or forgot my place, but the reflection in the hearts of others.

B y the age of eleven, I was thrilling crowds with my displays of legerdemain, captivating them with my voice and music, as well as horrifying them with my face. My exhibitions as The Living Death had become more than a parade of a pathetic little boy who looked like a corpse. I became more: a musician and a magician in my own right. Or that was at least what I fancied myself, and it brought me a measure of comfort and pride.

There was so much more I could be though, I knew it. I wanted more. I wanted to be free as I had been as a child. And I wanted to do more than play music, I needed to create it for myself. Mozart was composing symphonies and entertaining the crowned heads of Europe at my age. I was behind, but I could catch up. My first efforts at composition were juvenile and derivative, but they were *something* and they were mine.

Things were always changing at Steiner's museum of curiosities. Performers moved in and out, never staying for too long, while those of us who believed we couldn't leave felt trapped forever. Yet we changed too.

The year I turned thirteen, Gus died suddenly. A strongman joined the troupe and took to Rose. He was huge, with a great mustache and a voice that boomed like thunder. I think I hated him at first, for taking the attention of the one person that cared if I lived or died. His name was Gregory and he was tied to Steiner through debt. But he stayed because of Rose and married her. Or tried to. I don't know if it was legal or sanctified. It didn't matter. They had love in a way I couldn't understand.

I turned more to Sebastian after their union. I don't know if I could call him a friend, but he smiled when I sang. My voice eased him away from madness the way it had done for my mother. I played him my compositions, noting which ones made him laugh, which ones agitated him. Sometimes I would catch sight of Constance out of the corner of my eye and see that I had made her weep.

I sang or played to anyone who would listen in those days. It was the only way I wanted to be perceived: through music. When I sang, I could be beautiful and make all my sadness and loneliness and pain into the sweetest melodies. I sang to anyone and everyone, from the audience that came to gape at me to the silent gravestones and starry sky, hoping I would be truly heard. I think, looking back now, that I hoped if I sang long enough or loud enough, maybe fate or God or someone who could change things would hear me and give me a new life. But it never happened. Constance wept when my voice gave her poor brother a measure of peace, but it changed nothing. I had continued to change though.

I was no longer a child, and it was also because of Constance that I learned, to my dismay, what it meant to feel the desires of a man. I don't know if a person walking down the street would stop to admire Constance for her beauty. Her hair was light brown, the color of a rabbit's fur, and her eyes were blue and reminded me of the sky I so rarely got to see. Her body was soft and curvaceous, and when she performed, she rouged her cheeks, cinched her corset, and lowered her neckline to catch the attention of the audience. To a young man, who had seen few other women in his life, she was captivating.

There was also just her indomitable strength and determination to protect herself and Sebastian. The same strength that kept me at a safe distance. The first time she caught me staring at the way her breasts bulged from her corset when she was prepared to go on stage, she sneered and told me I'd have better luck with another corpse. Being a teenage boy on the precipice of peak adolescent idiocy, I was undeterred.

I knew she would never let me touch her, even though she treated her brother with such care, but I could look. Looking was exciting all on its own. A week later, I caught her (perhaps with some intention on my part) washing alone and singing to herself. I watched in awe as she took off all her clothes but her chemise and when she began to remove it, I was so startled I knocked over a pile of boxes in the hall where I was hiding.

She stopped singing and laughed – I still remember how enticing that sound was – then began again. When I dared to look once more, her whole glorious body was bare and the reaction it caused in my anatomy was so shocking and unexpected that I ran from the sight. Her laughter followed me into the shadows as I tried frantically to make *it* go down and discovered the pleasure that could bring. It was a gift of sorts, I think, and I was grateful.

There were a few days in my juvenile lust that I mistook my feelings for love, but Constance, with her grit and aloofness, didn't let that idea take root for long. Still, I jealously came to hate the nights when she'd go into Steiner's rooms. I learned from Ezra what it was they were doing, how it was Constance's way of keeping herself and her brother safe. I understood, but it still made me sick to think of it.

Once, I snuck close to listen. I thought it might make me hard to hear the sounds of her feigning pleasure as that awful man fucked her. It only made me sick and furious. That fury turned into a bout of defiance. I refused to perform the next night, and that earned me a thorough beating from Steiner and a stint in the torture chamber.

I looked at myself in those mirrors for the first time without screaming. How awful was I that a woman would choose a beast like Steiner over showing me more than an ounce of care? I was cursed and repulsive. I'd never know a lover's touch. At least not as long as I was no more than a powerless monster in a cage. I could impress audiences with my skill or my voice, but in the end, that was all I was: a thing with a terrible face to be locked away, whipped, and degraded.

By the time I was fourteen, I could have run. I had grown tall, and strong for my size. I was smart too, and I knew it. So smart it scared Steiner. It took more to bring me to heel after years in the cellar and on the stage had hardened me. The threat of the torture chamber could keep me in line, yes, but not always. Even there I knew I could sing and I knew I could dream.

I did dream of the wide world, the way my mother had at the same age, on the border between child and adult. But I had already been torn from the only home I'd ever known once. I was afraid to leave again and start anew. The only thing more frightening than the world I knew, was the one I didn't.

But I had started to dream, started to hope that I could be something out there in the wide world. If I was to find a new life, one day, I was sure what I wanted it to be. I wanted to be a composer. Or prove that I already was one. So the idea seized me to do just that.

My music had improved in my years of obsessive study and practice. In the dark, I had toiled away and penned a concerto. I thought was perfect for the orchestra next door, whose music had nourished and sustained me for years. I spent weeks perfecting my notation and scoring before I made my move and left the piece with the conductor.

Of course, I didn't give it to him directly. I snuck in at night through my secret path and left it on his podium with a note. I knew my penmanship left much to be desired, but surely the music would speak for itself! He would hear it and know *me*, know that we were alike and that I was more than the terrible shell I had been cursed with.

I don't know if he laughed when he looked at it. In my nightmares after he certainly did. What he did do with the music was worse: he took it back to Steiner. That was the final straw. Steiner decided he'd had enough of my defiance.

Steiner saw how I was growing and knew he couldn't keep me trapped longer or hurt me like before. So he turned to a new tactic to punish and control me, to remind all of us what we were to him: nothing more than things, exhibits to be controlled and replaced. He would hurt the most innocent and defenseless of us to make his point, especially to me. The guilt I felt was only matched by my fear.

He hauled me and Sebastian onto the stage and began to beat the poor boy, telling me to watch, telling us all to watch. He'd kill him if he wanted, he could kill any one of his freaks if we didn't obey. Constance ran in, screaming at Steiner to let her brother go. I begged for the same. We all did, but Steiner wouldn't stop with his whip. Sebastian had never possessed the gift of words, but he begged too in grunts and piteous groans. And then Constance threw her knife into Steiner's shoulder, staying his hand before he could strike her brother again.

It was chaos after that. The guards Steiner employed set upon us, and Steiner, wounded in the shoulder, went after Constance. She was fierce, but he was furious. Sebastian screamed like nothing I had heard before when he saw his sister fall under Steiner's hands. I pulled a guard off him and Sebatian grabbed an oil lamp then threw it towards the man who had made our lives hell.

All theaters, from the most decrepit to the grandest in the world, have the same enemy: fire. There is not a city in Europe that doesn't have a tale of a huge palace of dreams destroyed by a single spark. Steiner's theater would meet the same inevitable end.

The fire spread in the blink of an eye, racing up the curtains, consuming rotting beams and exploding every light and lamp it found. The guards and my compatriots in bondage ran, but Steiner, Constance, and Sebastian remained. And so did I. Sebastian screamed for his sister, and I jumped over the flames to where Steiner was still trying to strangle Constance, hearing my mother's screams under my father's fists. Suddenly, I had Steiner's fine coat clasped in my fists as I hauled him back and threw him. He flew so easily across the stage then through a wall of flames.

For so many years, Steiner had yelled to the crowd from that stage. "Come and see! The soul spat back into its corpse from hell! The apprentice of the devil! The ugliest face you will ever look upon!" I'll remember the echo of those words and that hateful voice until hell takes me back for good. And I'll take comfort in the knowledge that the last I heard of Steiner was him screaming over the roar of the flames as he died.

I was free of Steiner and his theater of humiliation and pain at last. We all were.

# 3. Travelling Song

*"Were you happy that he was gone?"*
*"I don't think happy is the right word. His death meant there would be*
*no more pain, nor tortures, nor terrible displays against my will. But it*
*also meant there was no one to tell me what to do with myself."*
*"Freedom like that when you've never had it is terrifying."*
*"Indeed it is."*

It was the spring of 1859 that Steiner died and we all were free. I was fourteen and had been in his clutches for six years, nearly half my life. Then suddenly, he was gone.

I had never thought much about my future when I was in Steiner's theater. There had been vague dreams, of course; of freedom and captivating the world with song. Of showing everyone who had rejected me that I was not the monster I seemed. The foolish dreams of a child, but nothing more than that.

With our jailer dead and our home in ashes, we were all abruptly faced with the question of our future. We were free of Steiner, yes, but none of us freaks could ever be free of what we were, nor the harm he had done by telling us there was only one thing we could be. There weren't many normal jobs for people like us, so most everyone set off looking for another freak show that would pay better and abuse less.

I tried to convince Constance and Sebastian that they didn't have to live that way anymore. They could be free to go anywhere. She told me I was a fool before they left, bound for America in the hopes that the great circuses there would take them on. I hope they found their way somewhere safe.

Rose and Gregory were the only ones that decided to try for a normal life, somewhere to the west. She refused the idea of America. She didn't want to return to the country that had sold her as a commodity and still believed (at least half of it) that she could be sold again. They offered to let me come with them. Well, Rose did, but I said no. I wanted freedom. I wanted to see the wide world beyond the cages I had been kept in for so long.

I wanted that, even though I knew I didn't belong in that world and never had. No place existed where I could stay and be safe. I was still a freak, still a monster whose face made people scream and faint, but I had skills and talent and wits too. I was in the twilight between boy and man, at an age where most boys think they are invincible. I could travel, but I needed a guide. So I went to the only people who might possibly take me in with them and whose path would take them far from Vienna and the possibility of being blamed for Steiner's death. I went to the Roma.

The Romani people had been forced to the edges of society for centuries. Vilified and blamed for every misfortune, they were enslaved or driven away, marked by their skin and ways as *other*, and always on the move. I had always felt a kinship with them, foolish as that was, and so, after days of wandering the alleys of Vienna, stealing food and hiding from the sun, I found a caravan at the edge of the city.

I knew a few of them from the theater; Ivo, who had taught me to play the violin, and who accompanied a man named Florian who danced with his wife Nina. I had always loved to watch them, the swish and swirl of Nina's layers of colored skirts and shawl, the stomp of Florian's rapid feet. However, it was a different thing for me to approach the circle of wagons than for them to see me in the city. I was the interloper. I was that thing that was unclean. I was *marime*.

The Romani people are not lawless; quite the contrary. Their rules and ways are closed, kept secret from the outside world and anyone who is not of the People: the *gaje*. The outsiders. There is nothing more important in those laws than remaining clean, for it keeps the balance between death and life, dark and light. Avoiding *marime* – uncleanness – is paramount to the People, and many customs exist to preserve that state.

The clothes from the lower half of a Rom's body could not touch those from the top in the wash, one could not eat from the same plate as *gaje*, for they did not know or honor the laws that kept pollution at bay, and women were secluded after childbirth and during menstruation, the most unclean of states. It was as unclean to touch the dead or to consort with their spirits, as for a woman's skirts to touch a man. In fact, a woman had the power to mark a man as *marime* just by hitting him with her skirt.

I was an outsider, unclean by my very nature, and I had the face of death, so I was even more suspicious. But I came to them with humility. I didn't ask to be part of their band, just for the right to follow them and share their fire once in a while. I swore I would earn my place.

It was not Ivo or Florian who spoke up for me, but Nina. She made the case that I could be useful as well as profitable. It was good, she said, to have a boy at hand who was *marime* in his very blood and who could touch those things they could not. If I was already polluted, and it didn't matter if I was polluted more by taking a message to a woman in monthly seclusion or removing the body of a dead thing. So I found a place; among them but not one of them. I found my usefulness.

The caravan traveled northeast out of Vienna, away from the walls of the city and into the woods and the wild, through farmland and hills. For the first time in my life, I was able to travel during the day, outside in the light. I hid myself as well as I could from the light and the perception of others even so. I wore a mask of cured leather and preferred to dress all in black with a hooded cloak – all the better to be a shadow. Steiner had forced me to keep my dark hair short so nothing could hide my face, and the memory of his shears against my skull inspired my resolve to let my hair grow as long as I could tolerate it.

I kept to the back of the group, so I could slip away once in a while. I'd linger in a quiet glen or by a stream and take off my mask. I'd let the sun see my ruined face and I learned what warmth and light really meant. The sun and moon and stars see all and do not judge, nor do the trees and rivers and rocks. And I loved them all.

After a few days, we came to Prague. That was the way of the caravan, to move from one city to another to find work for a while before moving on to the next place, in a great circle that intersected with the routes of other bands and clans. I thought in those early days that it must be hard, to not have a home, to always be moving. I told Ivo this, at the fire one night outside the walls of Prague, and he laughed. He told me that he was not homeless; in fact, he was luckier than the *gaje* whose houses could burn or who could be driven off their land like cattle.

Ivo explained that, for the Romani, home was not a place, nor a land; home was the People – the Roma. Home was the tight-knit families that made up the caravan, the music and the spices of their food, their laws and faith, the culture and ways they had carried with them and preserved for centuries.

"Where is your home, Erik?" he asked me. "Where are you at peace?"

I picked up the violin beside me and gave my answer: music. That was the thing that had always protected me. It was the home I carried with me when I had nothing else.

The music of Prague was different from Vienna's, but just as glorious. So too was everything about the "City of a Hundred Spires." For the first time in my life, I was free to explore and learn there to my heart's content with no fear of consequences. I performed in fairs and markets for money, sometimes with the Roma, sometimes on my own.

I beguiled the crowds with my voice and terrified them with my face only when they had given me all the coins I demanded of them. Some days though, I wasn't the center of attention and I still found my coins.

It was a brother and sister, Radu and Vadoma, who taught me to pick pockets. It wasn't honest work, but when the *gaje* only employed Roma for a few things, there was a need. Feeding a family and keeping the caravan secure were more important than the laws of the men who had treated the Romani people as outcasts for all their history.

I took to the skill instantly and with no remorse. I too was owed these coins and trinkets by the rich men who would as soon see me in a cage or take everything from a mother or a family without a thought. Each time I plucked a purse from another unsuspecting victim, I was striking a blow against... something.

It was the first time I'd had money of my own (well, mostly my own), and with those coins I bought the most precious thing in the world: knowledge.

I bought books on the city, books of history, books on music and art – anything I could find. I tore through them, selling them back to shops when I was done. I was soon able to afford a tent and an old mule to carry my belongings, but if I had kept every book I bought, I think the weight would have killed the poor beast. In German, French, English, and Latin, I read. And I explored.

I still preferred to move at night, for I hated the way people looked at my mask and the suspicion in their eyes. At night it was easier to pretend I was normal; just a person like anyone else.

But I wasn't like anyone else. I was beginning to realize that, even without my face to exclude me from the ranks of my fellow men, I was different. I could sing like the heavens, and any instrument I played was equally as blessed. I was intelligent, not just for my age, but for any man. I could learn fast, faster than was normal or natural. I took effortlessly to the most obscure or deviant of skills – magic and thievery – making myself silent and unseen.

It was in Prague that I found a new love as well. I had heard opera in Vienna, through walls and glimpsed through peepholes. But it was not until Prague, my pockets heavy with ill-gotten gains, that I could buy myself a ticket. It wasn't a grand opera – a boy in mismatched clothes and a mask would never have been admitted to the elite theaters, no matter how much I paid. But I was able to afford a place high in the top balcony of one of the smaller theaters.

I picked my first opera carefully, knowing that it was in this city that my beloved Mozart had found success with some of his greatest works, and so my first night in the audience was for the greatest of those masterpieces: *Don Giovanni.*

I cannot express the way that night changed me. That music took me to the heights of heaven as I watched the Don be dragged to the depths of hell. It was everything I had dreamed and more, a whole world created on that stage and brought to life with the magic of sound and theater. I gasped at the seductions, fumed at the injustice, and thrilled at the final moments of damnation.

I left that theater with my brain afire, as if the crucible of that music had reforged me into a new being. Could *I* ever create something so glorious? I had to, even if it was impossible for a monstrous boy who lived among the outcasts and the unwanted. But Don Giovanni himself had not let anything stop his desires or pursuits. In the face of death itself, he had refused to surrender. I could refuse my damnation as well. I could rewrite the story for the villain, with the right music. One day, I could give Don Juan his triumph.

But not yet. I was talented, I knew it, but I did not have an opera in me worthy of the idea. It would take time, and I thought, as all young people do, that time was something I had in abundance.

We moved on from Prague after a few months, east toward Nuremberg. Again I had a new city to explore, new crowds to entertain, and new knowledge to drink in. The Roma had begun to welcome me more, even a few times allowing me to eat with them, as long as I did not touch the same food as the men. But I scared them too. Ivo did not trust a boy who could play the fiddle with skill it had taken him decades to reach, and Florian became furious when he heard I had not only dared to talk to his sister when she was in seclusion but had offered to teach her to read. I knew my time with that caravan was ending, but luckily, we met another.

This clan was headed to Munich and they saw the utility of inviting me to join them. I was a good performer and a useful member of the group. I said my goodbyes and took my things and my poor, confused mule (I had named him Leporello by then) and joined the new caravan.

We went to Munich, another city of surpassing beauty and ancient stories. And there I began again as I had in Prague, learning all I could, listening to every note of music I could manage, living free.

It was in Munich one night, as I snuck into their great opera house to hear the genius of Wagner for the first time, that I realized for the first time in my life I'd found something akin to happiness.

There were no beatings or cages or tortures anymore. I did manage, once in a while, to find myself in a scrap, but I was strong now, fast and ruthless, and when someone tried to hurt me, they found themselves hurt much worse in return. People still screamed at me, but it was only when *I* chose. I had no home or family, but at least I had people among the Roma who would treat me with respect and welcome me for a while. But it was freedom that truly brought me joy. I could go anywhere I wanted. I could learn about anything that took my fancy. Everywhere I went, I could find music and survive.

It was ephemeral, of course, the joy I found in those years, but happiness always is. I think how scarce joy had been in my youth made the moments I found it later in life all the more precious. I found joy wandering the woods for days and cataloging the stars. I found it when a Roma silversmith took me on as an apprentice for a month and taught me the inner workings of watches and mechanics. I found it in learning new tongues and devouring the stories of new lands. I found it with each new composer I encountered or work of art I could take in. I was ugly and outcast, but the world was still so full of beauty that I could touch and share.

For three years, I crisscrossed the west of Europe, my thirst for knowledge and new wonders unquenchable. I traveled with the Roma when I could, slowly learning their language and traditions well enough that I could gain the trust of a caravan easily. I was never adopted into a family, as did happen with *gaje* children sometimes. My closeness to death itself made me forever unclean, but I was regarded after a while as someone who moved between the worlds.

It was usually the musicians who allowed me to join a caravan. I learned the most from them, and eventually, I was given the honor of learning their most sacred and treasured pieces, airs on the fiddle that told ancient tales. "The Resurrection of Lazarus" was my favorite among them.

I do not know if it was the moments of happiness or the melancholy and loneliness that followed them that encouraged me to dream. I was still young and foolish, and in my heart despite knowing what I was, I hoped that one day I would truly find a home beyond the songs I carried with me. I would meet people, and for a little while they would feel like friends, but there was always a moment when they would ask to see me or go somewhere in the world of light and the living that I simply could not follow. Soon after that, they would be gone.

Even free, I couldn't truly walk in the world of regular men with my mask. No matter how I tried to make it look like a real face, it still betrayed me. I enjoyed the winters, when I could cover myself in scarves and a hood and I could walk about without being stared at. That illusion died whenever it was time to step inside by the fire, so my hopes remained in the cold. That was until I found a place where I could wear a mask all day and still frolic among normal women and men. I went there just after I turned seventeen, when my Italian was good enough to pass for a local. I went to the masked revels of Venice at Carnivale.

I had never seen anything like Venice in the weeks before Lent. The city itself was a wonder, a miracle of architecture and empire, held aloft above her lagoon with nothing but faith in her own grandeur. *La Serenissima*, The Most Serene, she was called; but there was nothing serene about the chaos and debauchery of Carnivale.

The entire city donned masks and dominos, and for the first time in my life, not only could I just walk about like a normal man, but I could join in the celebrations and gaiety. I performed on the streets, amazing the crowds with my illusions and voice, and, oh, the unbridled glee I felt to have such freedom and acceptance at last. I cut quite a figure: taller than most men, thin and lithe as a bare tree in winter, swathed in my black cloak and wearing my white mask.

Within a day, I had earned invitations to a dozen parties among the elite of the city. The first such party I went to was so loud and bright it overwhelmed my senses. I wasn't used to having so many people so close to me or being in the center of such a cacophony. I nearly fled from the villa, but someone handed me a glass of wine and I learned exactly why men enjoy the gift of Dionysus.

In that raucous, madcap week, I learned to drink as well as carouse and laugh and frolic among people. I dazzled them with my skills, entertained them with my wit, and found myself much richer when I left thanks to the pockets I managed to pick. I was delirious with the pleasure of it all and amazed by the hedonism. At one party, there were women and men still masked but otherwise nude, set about the villa as living statues who came to life with a touch to their bare skin. Hours later, the celebration transformed into a true bacchanal, with bodies of all shapes and types joining together in unbridled lust.

I did not partake, though I considered it. I was too terrified of being found out as a monster, or letting anyone see or touch my body, scarred as it was from Steiner's abuses. But oh, the things I saw. I was amazed at the sheer variety of ways people could take pleasure, and the combinations it came in.

I saw a man and woman rutting on a table while another man simply kept on with his dinner. In the room next door, two women practiced pleasure on a silken divan while across the hall, one man penetrated another as a woman clapped and whooped next to them in encouragement. Further on, I found myself watching a woman caught between two men still in their masks. She seemed to find immense pleasure in taking two cocks at the same time, one from behind and the other in her mouth. I don't think they minded their audience or that I brought myself to a quick and breathless climax watching them lose themselves.

The next day, nursing the worst hangover of my life, the part of me that had wanted to throw myself into that orgy seethed with anger for not doing more. Despite my fears, my lust had been ignited as never before, and more than that, satisfying my desires wasn't a fever dream. For the first time in my life, I felt like it was possible that I might know the touch of another. Even though it made fear crackle under my skin to imagine such intimacy, my cock's desires were stronger. Wallowing in regret for all I didn't do in that villa, I resolved to make the last day of Carnivale count.

I was a performer at the party in a fine villa near the Grand Canal. The lady of the house had seen me two nights before and wanted the magician with the voice of an angel for her own soirée. It was crowded and close and loud, but the wine never stopped flowing, and as I poured more and more down my throat, it dulled my senses and anxieties.

I held nothing back in my performance, treating the crowd to illusions that made them squeal in delight before I took a place behind the pianoforte and played and sang like never before. Was this how Liszt felt when he drove crowds wild, I wondered? It was ecstasy to hear them cheer for me and I loved every second.

The hostess was in rapture, plying me with drink and praise and before I knew it, she pulled me from the party into her private rooms. She was older, I could tell from how she spoke, and her honeyed words were as delightful as the love of the crowd or the sweet, sedating wine.

"I have never heard such a genius! Are you sure you are not a great composer hiding in my house?" she said to me. "Or are you the devil come to steal our souls?"

I laughed and drained a glass and told her I was just a man. When she reached under my domino to confirm that was true, my cock stood immediately to attention. "Surely a man as talented as you must have other skills?"

"I've never had occasion to practice," I heard myself say, the wine speaking for me above my panic as she touched me. She laughed so heartily at that, her breasts barely contained by her costume, her neck so long and beautiful.

"I shall have to teach you, young man."

The wine and my surging lust made the world spin as she pulled me to her bed and discarded enough of her clothes that I could grip her sumptuous breasts and gasp at the heat of her desire when she put my trembling hand on her sex. I didn't need any more encouragement, my body took over, led by my cock, and I found myself plunging into her before I could even think.

It felt so good, so warm and welcoming. For a few moments, I was as human and alive as anyone else, pleasure coursing through me and overcoming me. I was clumsy and inept, but neither of us cared. She made noises that told me she enjoyed having me in her, delightful little gasps and coos as I fucked as her hard and fast as I could. Lust and wine spurred me forward until the orgasm took me, a symphony of sensation compared to the brief melodies I'd experienced courtesy of my own hands.

I fell onto her bed in a daze, relaxed and satisfied as I had never been before in my life. I remember she laughed and said something about how I was not done while she remained unsatisfied, and that it would not do to have a mask on for my next lesson. All of a sudden, I felt fresh air on my cheek and the room was filled with her screams. All my pleasure and contentment were replaced with terror.

I jumped off the bed, hiding my face, desperate to retrieve my mask and make her stop screaming. She threw things at me, she called me a demon, and I found myself frozen in fear, huddled in the corner of that opulent bedchamber, just a child again faced with my mother's madness and violence. All I wanted was for her to stop. I begged her to stop. Then a man burst in.

"What did you do to my wife?" he bellowed before turning to see me. He was drunk too. I could see it in the flush of his unmasked face. "Did you fuck this monster, you whore?" he demanded of the woman who had taken my virginity. And it was her he went after, not me. I don't know why. I don't know if she had cuckolded him before or if he was simply a brute, but he fell upon her with a fury that made her scream anew.

It wasn't a fair fight. He grabbed her and struck her again and again while I shouted at him to stop, my hatred for cruel men overcoming my fear of being seen. I grabbed at him from behind and someone screamed, her or me, I can't even say. But the husband didn't like that and so he threw his wife across the room, rough and hard. And at the perfect angle so that she hit her head against the marble top of her vanity.

She was dead before she hit the floor. I can still see the way her skull caved in...the bright red of her blood as it gushed onto the inlaid wood floor. It was different from what my mother had looked like dead on the ground because of a brutish man and her monstrous son, but it was also exactly the same. But this time, I wasn't a child.

The husband turned on me, ready to blame me for the murder he had just committed. I knew right then I was already condemned. I can't say how I won that fight, but the thought that I had nothing to lose gave me strength, along with the righteous inferno of my anger. I had never hated a stranger so much. I can't remember what his face looked like because he was Steiner all over again, with his fists and mirrors. He was my father, another monster who cast a woman aside to her death.

I ended it with my hands on his neck. He tried to pry me off – struck at my arms and clawed my hands as I choked him. I felt entirely sober as I watched his face turn red and his eyes roll back, as he sputtered and flailed as I squeezed his last breath from him. He went limp, and I kept choking him until I was sure he was dead, power and triumph coursing through me. And then, just like the glow of the pleasure from before, it was gone.

Suddenly I could hear the commotion of the party still going on downstairs and I saw clearly where I was: in the center of a scene of a double murder. I ran.

When I'd been the cause of my mother's death, there had been nothing but numb shock, then grief. With Steiner, it had felt like triumph and justice. This felt like both at the same time, and yet so different.

I'd been defending myself. I had no choice. I didn't seek out a man to kill that night. It wasn't my fault. I told myself all of that over and over as I vomited into a canal. I believed it by the time I fled the city. Once I reached Rome, days later, I knew he had deserved it.

I had known since I was able to reason that I was different, that I was cursed and marked by death. It changed everything and nothing to know that I had the capacity to take a life and that murder had come so easily to my hands. I was unclean in every way, just as the Roma believed. I avoided the People for months out of respect, unwilling to taint any clan on accident until I could be somewhat cleansed or absolved. I found distraction in Italy while I lingered and hid from anyone who might hunt me down for my crime.

The wonders and history of Rome proved a more than adequate distraction, as did her music. I loved the ruins and the architecture and I came to be fascinated by the engineering feats of the ancient emperors and modern masters. But Rome was just the beginning. My true passion for what men could build was born in Florence, under the impossible heft of Brunelleschi's Duomo.

I had been to many cities by that point, all beautiful in their own ways, but Florence was special. Every corner was a work of art, every street held memories and history hundreds of years old. I spent months there, reading and learning from any builder who I could ply with wine to talk to a young man in a mask for an hour or so. But even in a place that beautiful, I could not stay. I was marked like Cain, and I knew ill fortune would befall if I stayed anywhere too long.

Perhaps all my time with the Romani people had affected me, and like them, I chaffed at staying in one place for more than a season. I finally met a band near Naples that summer. Their wise woman saw something in my eyes and looked at my hands, but I spoke their words and bowed my head and asked for a place by the fire. She purified me with smoke and water, and I again began to travel with the People.

My heart didn't need the spell. I knew the truth of myself and accepted it. I felt no more guilt or shame for what I had done than for what I was by my very nature...The Living Death. Erik, a changeling child, a curse.

# 4. Rondo à l'Est

*"There are only a few ways to live when one is cursed."*
*"Are there now?"*
*"One can run from fate, or one can accept it and embrace it."*
*"There is another way, you know. You can break it."*

In the final years of my teens, I traveled all of Europe and the Mediterranean, following the same pattern everywhere I went. I would find a great city – I liked cities far more than backwards villages – and I would lose myself to it until I had nothing left to give or take. In cities, there are always places where the undesirables are tucked away by those in power. Ghettos and closed districts, underground worlds, sewers and alleyways: all the places on the edge of civilization where the outcasts hide. Such areas can be dangerous, but I had learned by then that I was dangerous too.

I would explore, usually at night, taking in every sight and wonder I could. From the mosaics of the Alhambra to the pyramids at Giza, from the ruins of Athens and Ephesus to the Great Synagogue of Budapest, I would listen to every sound and song along the way. Knowledge and music were my greatest joys. I would buy books and spend days in whatever rooms I'd managed to find reading, only to emerge to earn money for food and more knowledge and exploration.

I was good at getting money however I chose to do it. It was never hard for me to draw a crowd with my voice or playing on the violin (or whatever instrument I found convenient). Wearing a mask always meant people asked to see my face, but only sometimes would I oblige. It depended on the foulness of my mood and the depth of my audience's pockets. No matter what, I hated it.

It always left me feeling violated and flayed when I did it, each time more than the last. Even after years of freedom, the memories of Steiner's whips and tortures and the screams of his audience had not dulled. I heard them louder in my memory each time a new crowd screamed at the sight of my corpse's face.

Sometimes, I'd need days to recover, hiding wherever I could find that was close and dark where the screams and noise of the world didn't echo so loud in my ears. I'd wrap myself in heavy blankets, blot out any outside light, and turn to music or books to recover before going out again.

This was why I preferred other ways of making money: namely, taking it from those who had too much of it. One thing I found in every city, along with the people who had been pushed to the margins, were the rich, heartless ones doing the pushing. Hating the upper classes was in my blood, passed down from my mother who had grown up watching the English drain her country dry while her people starved. I found no irony in having inherited the blood of nobility from my other parent. I hated myself quite thoroughly, so it felt just.

The rich and the elite were everywhere I went: at the operas and parading down the streets, blind to the suffering they caused all around them. I had no compunction about picking their pockets or palming the jewels off their wrists. It was a game, really, one I always got to win, and I enjoyed every moment I played it. It felt like striking a righteous blow against them.

I was good at striking real blows as well. I had been a skilled fighter for years, if only because I needed to be to survive. Living in the places I did, how I did, and with the face I had was a violent business.

I didn't kill for years after Venice, but the knowledge that I could made me a dangerous man. I tried to make myself look as unapproachable as possible as well, draping myself in black, wearing my hair long to cover my mask. And even with all of those defenses, I found myself in fights, perhaps more frequently than the average deformed bastard magician wandering the backstreets of the world.

I wasn't entirely innocent when it came to how those fights started, I will admit. I may have perhaps encouraged the impatience and annoyance of others by stealing from them or calling them idiots. But can you blame me when so many of them *were* idiots? I was just being honest. The men I provoked were fools and bullies, and when we fought, it gave me such satisfaction to flatten them to the floor and leave them shocked and bleeding. It took me until my twenties (and one or two stabbings) to learn that this was a way of making money too.

I liked fighting in the pits and dirty arenas of the seediest places I could find. I wore a black mask tight on my face. People cheered for me differently in those bouts, bloodthirsty and wild, and it was a new kind of thrill to pummel the brutes who were foolish enough to step into the ring with The Living Death. Taking off my mask to shock my opponent felt like cheating, but it was the only way of unmasking myself that didn't make my skin crawl, because I could quench my panic with violence and the coins I won.

That was the only way I touched people, with my fists or to steal a bauble from the neck or wrist. After my experience with the flesh in Venice, my appetites were more than curbed. I still looked, of course – still desired. There were always places where you could pay a few coins to see some flesh without being touched, and without even being seen yourself. I visited such establishments a few times, watched a few fleshy displays of skin and skill, but it felt empty. If I had desires, my own imagination and hands were sufficient, and I had no inclination to seek out more.

I tried to convince myself that sexual pleasure was of no interest to me, not that I knew any whore I paid to pleasure me might be cursed by touching me or might refuse. Or that the idea of being touched made me want to wretch and crawl out of my skin in panic. It was boring, I said, when acquaintances asked. I lied.

There were many other pursuits for a ravenous mind like my own aside from the flesh, including those of the spirit. I was an eternal student, always looking for something new to learn that might excite me or reveal the mysteries of the universe. I studied magic for that reason, not the tricks and illusions I'd perfected as a teenager, but (allegedly) real magic from alchemists and mystics wherever I could find them.

I met mediums who said they talked to the dead. One offered me a hundred gulden to pretend to be a ghost for a séance. I took it, of course, and pulled off my performance as dear departed Uncle Leo quite well, if I do say so myself. I learned herbs from wise women and drank in every story I could of the Good Folk, demons, and the creatures of the night.

I had been looking for ghosts since I was a child in that churchyard. It wasn't until Poland that I met one. It wasn't midnight, nor was it in a cemetery. I was in a library at three in the morning. I had fallen asleep reading and woke to the sound of steps. It was a monk, walking slowly through the stacks, concerned that everything had been moved. I knew the moment I looked at him that he wasn't alive; maybe it was the way the air was cold or how he seemed only half there no matter how I stared at him. He looked at me and raised his finger to his lips before I could speak. Silence was important in a monk's library, though no monks had been there for three hundred years.

I wasn't scared at all, only disappointed he did not stay to talk. I guess he wanted silence.

I wanted music. No matter where I traveled, I wanted music. I continued to compose and play whenever I could, finding my freedom in the strings of my violin or the lilt of a piano. When I played, I was no longer a hideous, broken man striving to belong – I became those sounds. Through music I could exist beyond and outside my body, forgetting for a brief time about my curse. It was the same when I listened.

I heard all the greats of the first half of the century: from the charm of Schubert and the well-mannered beauty of Brahms to the bombastic fire of Berlioz and tearful melodies of Chopin. I loved it all, though some more than others.

I returned to Munich specifically to hear the premiere of Wagner's newest opus, *Tristan und Isolde*, in 1865. I had to hide in deep recesses above the stage to listen, for there were no tickets to be had, especially for someone like me. I stood for all four hours of that miraculous music, the mystic, unresolved "Tristan chord" tugging on my very soul so that I didn't even feel the aches of my body. There was only music; incredible, indelible music that transformed love and death into something utterly sublime, impossible to express with mere words.

Hidden in the shadows of the theater, I wept in awe and in jealousy. If a man with a character as detestable as Wagner's could create such beauty, surely there was hope for me... But where? How? And he was only tainted by prejudice and scandal, not by death itself like me. To be fair, the whole of world seemed tainted by death in the 1860s. I was not unique.

I encountered many wonders as I traveled, but I also encountered war and bloodshed, the sound of bombs or the echo of an army march often interrupting my travels. Usually they were Prussian. For the whole of the 1860s the great German commanders were set on forging a new power at the expense of the old ways and empires, and I had little desire to see it. All I saw of war was how the men in power threw their armies at each other like children playing chess, unconcerned with the bloodshed and suffering they caused.

After so many years, I grew tired of the so-called West. So I followed the caravans and traveled east, with many a detour along the way to learn at some new shrine of magic or knowledge. I traveled through Turkey and Anatolia, then down to the Holy Land. I continued south along the Red Sea, skirting the great Arabian desserts among the caravans, to many great cities, all the way to the tip of the peninsula.

It was a different world in so many ways: the music, the smells, even the color of the sun. And I did see the sun in the East more than I had before because there the women, and even some men, dressed in robes and veils that covered their faces. I understood, in my own way, how a face could be an afront to holiness. So I donned my own veil and walked the streets in woman's garb. I was a strange and tall woman, of course, but it is remarkable how women can be invisible to men when they are not the object of desire.

I walked the bazaars and winding streets and listened to music on instruments I had never encountered. I avoided others, but still managed to make a few acquaintances, but none so interesting to me as Maha, who I met in the port city of Salah.

Maha engaged me in conversation at the edge of a market. She noticed me admiring her eyes and told me that was what her name meant: beautiful eyes. Apt, was it not? That was why she had chosen it, she explained, and with a smile behind her veil and a glint in those onyx eyes, she confessed her name had once been Omar, when she had been born as a boy.

Maha made it sound like a simple mistake, or perhaps a trick of the *djinn*, I was never sure, but she had known as soon as it was possible to know that she was a woman despite her body, and once she could, she lived and dressed accordingly. She had met others, though they were few, who did the same. Her tale made me wonder how many I had met in my life that had similar stories hidden behind their own masks.

Women in the East, as much as the West, were seldom treated with the dignity afforded to men, and were denied freedom as well. To cover my face with a veil was to exchange one sort of mark as an outsider for another and mark myself as lesser than the men in power who set the standards. Such female disguises (though for Maha, it was not a disguise) were useful, but dangerous.

A few weeks after meeting her, I was on the same street as Maha when she was accosted by a trio of young, intoxicated men. They wanted to rape and rob, I could tell from where I hid, but then they quickly discovered Maha's secret and felt entitled to punish her blasphemy and deviance. I stopped them quite easily.

I had not killed since Venice. I did not think of myself yet as a killer, but that night, wanted to be. Maha stopped me, reminded me that we were in danger already and that three bodies left in the street could cost us both our lives. So we ran from that city to the port. Maha found space on a boat bound back in the direction I had already traveled, towards Jeddah. I was sad to see her go a different direction. It had been comforting to know someone so brave who still held such hope. I hope she is still alive somewhere, smiling at the world while her beautiful eyes glitter with light.

I took a different ship from Maha, bound east for Mumbai, or as the British on the vessel who thought they owned the placed called it, Bombay. The heat and the smells, the spices and crowds... It was a brave new world to be explored once again. Yet there was much familiar in India too.

I took quickly to learning the tongues (of which there were many), because they were so close to the language of the Romani. Indeed, it was not from Egypt that the Romani had traveled, as the *gaje* assumed, but from India long ago. There was new music and new poetry and new gods so ancient they felt familiar. As always, there were men with pale skin and cold eyes who cared only for their power and gold. I reached India in early 1867, nearly a decade after the British had taken the country for themselves and made every Indian a subject of their distant Queen.

Five thousand miles from the Irish villages where my mother had grown up watching her family's cows be sold to English lords while the peasants were left nothing but potatoes, I found myself once again in a land occupied by their Empire. It was not just an empire of armies and force, but an empire of money and exploitation. And while I quickly followed my usual patterns in Mumbai, I also soon found myself honing my other, more wicked skills with the oligarchs as my target.

The wounds in India from a failed and bloody rebellion ten years before were still fresh, and there were many across the provinces that had not given up the fight. Though in truth 'the fight' for many was simply an excuse to live outside the law and take that which they wanted or felt they deserved. I was not one to disagree with such reasoning.

I was twenty-two, and while I was unlike most men in a myriad of ways, I was also a typical young person of that age and thought I was invincible and that every thought that came into my head was correct. They were not, and I was not. I was about to learn that very painfully.

I traveled slowly inland from Mumbai, finding my way in with the criminals and worse than that in India, the Untouchables. The caste system, with its rigid divisions of society based on birth, fascinated me as much as the gods and goddesses with many arms and faces. I must admit, this idea that the lot one is dealt in this life is due to sins in the last, was strangely comforting to me. Was that why I had been born with such gifts and curses? Because my soul had committed some crime in the life before? Did that mean I had hope for the next?

It was refreshing to see a country filled with so many faiths. They did not always agree, but to be able to hear a call to prayer and a moment later walk by a temple to Elephant-headed Ganesh made me rethink my own conception of the divine. I had always thought myself a pagan of sorts, finding myself closest to what I would call God when I heard music, or looked up into a star-filled sky. I met Hindus, Jews, Muslims, Jainists, and more in India, as well as Sikhs, and I found myself in one of the Sikhs' holiest cities eventually.

Amritsar, Ambarsar, or even Rāmdāspur, depending on who you were speaking to, was the second-largest city in the province of Punjab, and one of those cities that teemed with such life it felt ready to explode. It was a hot bed for industry and all that went with that. Where there is money there is corruption and those who wish to spend said money in the worst ways. Often, they are the worst people. I found myself, among a group of men determined to take some small measure of compensation from one such oligarch. My fellow robbers reminded me exactly why I rarely worked with others. They were not only incompetent, but without honor.

I was abandoned by my compatriots and caught as we tried to steal back jewels that they claimed were their country's to begin with. But for my captor, Captain Pinkerton – a high-ranking director in the East India Company – that was only part of his income. Pinkerton had been a soldier, as you may have guessed from his insistence on being called Captain. He missed the fight, the blood and the chaos. So he had created his own version of war in a hidden enclave of the city, where he men in his employ or control fought for the amusement of screaming crowds.

I was well acquainted with underground fighting, as I have mentioned. Indeed, I fancied myself quite the adept. I had a particular recklessness when it came to my body. After all, what was more pain and another scar compared to everything I had experienced since birth? I was fierce, formidable, and steadfastly refused to die. So I came into that arena in Ambarsar full of arrogance. I told myself I could win my way out or, if needed, I could easily escape. I was quickly humbled.

This was blood sport like I had never seen, and I barely escaped my first match with my life. We were not allowed blades or clubs, but any other weapon was fair game, and the first man to beat me did it with nothing but the yellow turban unwound from his head. He was old, this man, at least sixty, but he was fast and snuck behind me. Before I could even turn, yellow silk flew through the air and wrapped around my neck. In seconds I fell to my knees, all blood and air cut off. I surrendered before I lost consciousness.

Surrender was allowed there, even encouraged. Finding warm bodies for the pits was hard some days, and Captain Pinkerton wanted to keep his money flowing and keep the crowd entertained. The Captain certainly didn't want me to die; it was too much of a draw to have a living corpse battling in his little arena, so I was marked to be spared. I must admit, looking back at that time and others, that my face has saved my life as much as it has endangered it.

I did see men die there though. On my third night, the man who had beaten me with a length of fabric garroted a man three times his size and half his age, snapping his neck with a flick of his wrist for good measure. I had to know the trick of this magical lasso the man wielded, so I approached him when we were confined to our dark, sweltering quarters.

His name was Nehal. According to some of his stories, he had been raised a criminal among a fraternity of stranglers, but other times he claimed he had been born on the streets of Lahore and fought his way into a band of highway robbers. However he came to join them, one thing that was true was his history with the infamous Thuggee.

The Thugs, as the British like to call them, were a popular tale told to frighten travelers and justify the empire's expansion. They were not, as widely reported, mad cultists sacrificing innocent merchants along the road to fearsome Kali. They were merely highway robbers, adept at quick strangulation, a technique which allowed them to ambush groups and pick them off one by one, because with one of their deadly lassos around your neck, you could not call for aid.

Nehal had survived the British purges of the Thugs years before but kept his length of catgut hidden in his turban, weighted on one end with lead. I hounded him for weeks to teach me to use it. When finally he relented, I caught on quickly. I was so enthralled by this innocent rope. It was more than it seemed, just as I was.

Pinkerton on the other hand, had grown tired of the thing. Nehal's fights were all over too fast, and the customers – all British officers and company men – came to watch the savages fight, not a one-sided battle they couldn't bet on because it was always over too quickly. They were berating Pinkerton one night after Nehal once again took down his man in a flash. Some colonel offered a hundred pounds to any man that would take the Thug's life, but none of us stepped forward. What use was money to prisoners and the unwanted?

So Pinkerton jumped into the ring, drew his gun, and shot Nehal in the chest, killing him in cold blood. When the crowd cheered, their hoots and wails sent me right back to Steiner's stage. These men were the monsters, not I nor the criminals they had created by hoarding everything to themselves and destroying anyone who was inconvenient.

I jumped into the ring and I heard gasps in the crowd at the sight of my hideousness. This time they were right to fear me. I was death made flesh, come to judge them all, and I reveled in it. I grabbed the lasso, watching the yellow silk of Nehal's turban fall from the catgut cord into his blood. Pinkerton could have shot me so easily, but he hesitated, wary of cutting off a source of money. It was his greed that killed him – I was just the instrument of fate. The lasso whipped through the air and in a blink, he was dead.

It started a riot for me to fell our jailer so easily. Chaos broke out and I fled into the night with the lasso in my hand. It rarely left my side for the rest of my travels, but it would be a few years still before it rendered another sacrifice to the Goddess of Death.

I continued my wanderings, ever moving east, first through the rest of India, and then into China, passing through vast, wild landscapes and cities like nothing I had encountered before. It was a new land of wonders, but I had started to grow tired.

I was tired and furious that however far I went, I would find the same things – the same wars for gold, the same Europeans scrambling for the riches of other lands while at home they squabbled over politics.

The British were in China too, a country they had forced open like an oyster to steal its pearls and take its money in the opium trade. It sickened me; how they had tricked a population into addiction and then fought wars when the Emperor had tried to stop their poisoned product's flow.

They had used their wars to steal an entire city, though it had not been much when they took it. Under their rule, Hong Kong had grown into a curious hybrid. It was not Chinese, not entirely, and the mainlanders did not see it as part of their own land anymore. But it wasn't British either.

The nights there were as raucous as the days, with markets only coming alive after sunset to deal in silks and trinkets and food of every kind. Tea houses and Maj Jong parlors lined the streets, altars adorned with fruits and incense sat outside businesses to bring good fortune. People did the same things as anyone else in the world. They built families and worked and danced and laughed, and at the end of the day, they went home.

For the first time in my life, I started to long for that as well. I had been wandering for over a decade, finding my home in music and magic and wonder. But music cannot welcome you in from the cold, bring you into a hearth, and give you rest in a familiar bed, where all is safe. I dreamed of a place like that for myself just like I dreamed of one day sharing my music with an adoring public. It was time to go home, but where was home?

Finding my way back to Europe was the easy part. Nearly every day, boats were loaded in the harbor at Kowloon under the shadow of Victoria Peak, and I found a secure place to stow away on in the night. The *Ceres*, it was called, and it was bound for England on a long voyage.

It was surprisingly easy to stay concealed in such close quarters for so long out at sea. I'd take the air at night and steal whatever I needed from the crew – food, books, and at least one cask of beer. The superstitious sailors soon all agreed that the *Ceres* was haunted. It made me laugh, and of course, I could not help but give the people what they wanted.

I enjoyed feeling the sea air on my face at midnight, and I also enjoyed the way the boatswain screamed and wet himself when he saw a skeleton in a dark cloak taking in the moonlight. By the end of the voyage, I was thinking back to my time with that medium as Uncle Leo, and I was terribly disappointed that there were not more careers available for ghosts.

To come from so many places where the British reigned to their home soil was strange. Their prim faces and stodgy accents were the norm in their isles, just like the rain and gloom. I do confess it was a relief to feel cold again after my time closer to the equator. It was also a shock, to come back to a place I had been as a child and see it with new eyes. This time, I took on London as a man, not a frightened boy.

It was a great city, I must admit, but the constant fog from the factories was as oppressive as the manners and morals of the British. Their queen sat in mourning in her great palace while children begged on the street and their empire grew ever greater. They were so nervous about everything from the rise of Prussian power to the influence of the debauched morals of the French.

There was music though: great organs and symphonies, operas and concerts. I found my way to them all and drank them in like I had found a spring in an oasis. I snuck into theaters and halls, pubs, and salons to listen and learn and be inspired. It was not just music I could enjoy in London, but the theater. I had read every work of Shakespeare long before, but even hiding in the flies, or with my face concealed by my mask and a scarf in a back row, it was a joy to see those great works performed before an audience.

Still, London was not my home. I wandered away after a few months, into the country, where I walked among the standing stones at Avebury and Stonehenge and felt their magic and mystery spark in my pagan heart. I offered them a sacrifice of song in the night and I felt them whisper back. Would they hear my prayers? Would any god care that for the hope I held and nursed to finally find a place to rest? I found my answer the next day when I met a band of Roma, bound north.

I stayed with them for months more, making our way towards Scotland. It was slow going and I liked it that way. They liked that I brought in audiences with my music and magic. I had learned a great deal from my fellow illusionists in the East, and I could do wonders with cards. cups and the occasional dove.

I was a sensation in the streets of Edinburgh when we arrived and I wondered if I could make a true return to the stage. That city was as haunted as any, full of scholars and doctors, poets and romantics, as well as grave robbers and fiends. I could make a name there, I thought: "Erik: The magician who sings like an angel." The crowds loved my voice and tricks, they could love my music too if they could just see past my face or never see it at all. Perhaps a music publisher might even look at my work.

That absurd dream got me as far as the office of an impresario. He thought I had talent but asked to see "the goods" before he booked me. My face, he meant. I froze when he asked, once again a frightened child in Steiner's torture chamber. The man used my hesitation to grab for my mask, and I'll never forget the look of horror on his face and my reflection in his eyes.

I broke his wrist without thinking, left him blathering there in his smoky office in the back of the theater. That look had been so familiar and awful. It meant I was still the monster, still cursed, and there was no home for me here either.

Maybe I'd find one in the place my mother had left.

Ireland has a great epic; *The Book of Invasions* it's called. It tells the tale of all the armies and peoples that came to Eire over the distant centuries and made it what it was. It's a myth, full of Fair Folk and gods in disguise, but it is apt that invasions and magic are foundations of the land.

I was enthralled as soon as I arrived there. The rain and the trees were like England's or Scotland's, and yet it was different. The language lilted and the sound of pipes and fiddles wafted from pubs with the smoke. It was a land they said was shaped by the work of giants and gods, full of blessed springs and green hills. Bright Brigid's sacred land. It was the place I had heard of in my mother's tales, and it felt like coming home.

It was different there, playing the violin and tin whistle for my bread. There I heard the musicians playing together in the pub, and I wanted to join. But I couldn't. There, when I dazzled a crowd with magic, they whispered that the Good Folk might have traded me off as a child. I hid the way it would send me into a cloud of pain and memory for days before I retreated. I composed a great deal there, and read, in my little rooms in inns along the road that I took under cover of night. From there I could hear the music from below, and it was enough to sing along alone.

It took me months to build up the courage to return to *her* village of Coolaney, to see if there was anyone with whom I shared blood who still lived there. Just the inquiry itself would be a problem. I had grown to dislike talking to people over the years. I wasn't good at it, you see. People said one thing and meant another, and while I knew in my mind that there was no trusting others, I still made the mistake of doing so over and over. I never knew what the right thing was to say or how to say it. In turn, people never trusted a man in a mask, and so that made it even harder to connect, if one could even call it that, with my "fellow man." The prospect of the conversations I'd need to have to find my family were daunting for all these reasons.

Still, I dared to talk to the man at the pub on the high street. It's always the man who pours the ale who knows all the stories. If you keep paying, he'll keep talking. He knew the name Gilbride, but as far as he knew all of that family had left Coolaney for America ten years before. The only thing I felt when I learned that was relief. What family would have wanted me anyway? They were lucky to be an ocean away.

I wandered from village to village, sometimes with other bands of travelers or Roma, but often on my own, watching as the seasons changed. And against every bit of advice my mother (and every person who wanted to keep their skin and soul also) had always told me, I would walk at night among the barrows and hills, where the Fair Folk were said to dance in their circles and lure travelers into bogs or the Otherworld.

There was part of me that wanted to test what my mother had said: that claim I was a changeling. Maybe I was. I swear I heard music sometimes in those wanderings. Beautiful tunes I could not place, along with the lights in the shadows that tempted me from my path. I followed them like a fool and found nothing. Even still, I kept looking, pulled by hope and fascination.

I went to the Cave of Cats in Roscommon on Samhain, the night when the doors to the Otherworld were said to open. I walked right into the gaping maw in the hill, said to be a door to the Fairy realm or hell, depending on who you asked. Would I finally find my home *there*?

The air seemed to whisper, though, and the song I heard was one my mother used to sing. *Siúil, siúil, siúil a ruin. Siúil go socar agus siúil go ciúin...*

I didn't wait for the night to be over. I left as fast as I could, the weight of years of grief choking the air from my lungs. It had been foolish to push myself closer to the place she had come from and that well of sorrow. I traveled as fast as I could back to Dublin and by the time I was there, I had set myself a new destination: the land of my birth, of the other half of my blood. I would return to France at the turn of 1869 into 1870. A new decade could be a new start.

Again, I was to be disappointed.

# 5. Variations sur La Marseillaise

*"You still wanted a home."*
*"I wanted more than that. I wanted a place where I was free to live as any*
*other man. I didn't want just a place in the world I had been born to, I*
*wanted to make a new one."*

S tepping back onto the soil of France was different than returning to England or Ireland. There was a sense of familiarity to everything, even though I had seen little of the landscape of France. I decided to change that. I spent weeks in Brittany first, traveling along the coast through villages of stone seemingly carved from the seaside cliffs. From there I joined a Roma caravan and traveled south, through Nantes and into Poitiers and La Rochelle.

France had changed since my youth. Emperor Napoleon III fancied himself a man of the future, and had set about modernizing the country, from agriculture to reordering the streets of Paris into a perfect model of efficiency and yet keep himself a king in a land that wanted freedom. The tides were changing in France; even I could feel it.

I circled the country in the first few months of 1870 until I finally set foot in Paris. I had seen a hundred great cities in my twenty-five years on the earth, but none set my mind and heart afire like Paris. It was the city of my dreams, bustling with art and industry. I found the underground half of the city easily, full of networks of tunnels and sewers where I could move undetected.

The city was mine that spring, and I sated myself on music, art, and literature to my heart's content, steadfastly ignoring the rumblings of war and chaos from the countryside. I despised the nobles and the Emperor who elevated them, but just like them, I remained confident in France's power on the world stage.

But the Empire had already failed. I saw that daily, as workers throughout the city toiled and strived for their bread while the rich rolled past in their carriages on the way to parade their wealth at the Opera. It was really an act of equalizing justice for me to attend the same performances without paying. I stole into the old theater on the *Rue Le Peletier* to hide in the wings or the highest loges. I found the French preference for mediocre composers like Meyerbeer and Halévy tiresome, but I marveled at the spectacle of it all. I hated how the rich would not stop their chattering in their boxes while the music played. I wondered if it would be any different at the new Opera that was to be the jewel in the Emperor's crown.

Napoleon III had employed Baron Georges-Eugène Haussmann to transform Paris. He had torn down everything old and decayed and remapped the city, filling it with perfectly straight avenues and hundreds of buildings of cream-colored stones and blue-iron roofs. At the heart of this grand plan was the *Avenue de l'Opéra*, running a straight line north-west from the Louvre up to the massive theater that was already being referred to as if it were a palace. There had been dozens of operas in the city over the years, but this was to be the one and only true Paris Opera House.

The first time I saw her was at dawn, as the rays of the sun from the east hit the great copper dome rounded in filigree like a crown. And, oh, what a queen she was, imposing and robust, ostentatious and aloof, full of dangerous secrets even then, when under construction. The Palais Garnier was meant to be a temple to art as well as a monument to the Emperor's power and greatness. I loved her for the former and hated that she would be used for the latter.

I saw my father in the face of every noble patron of the old Opera when I attended and I resented them more with each passing day. Maybe it was just being in France, walking by the *Place de la Concorde* where Madame Guillotine had done her bloody work cutting down the nobles less than a century before, only to see that they had sprung back like weeds.

I watched them laugh, I watched them frolic and I hated them like I had seldom hated anything before, save the curse of my own face. Being young, I thought I could turn my petty abhorrence into a crusade. I needed money, as always, and so rather than perform or, heaven forbid, work honestly for my own bread, I decided I would take what I deserved from them.

The Opera became my bait, and on the nights of the grand performances, I went to their manses in the *Faubourg Saint-Germain* and slipped in to pilfer jewels and whatever else I could carry. The booty was easy to sell in the seedier parts of the city. I was quite proud of my spoils and who I had stolen them from, so I bragged to my buyers.

They said I sounded like a Blanquist radical, as if I should know what that meant. That was how I first heard of the radicals that hated the Emperor and the rich more than I could ever imagine. The men who were prepared to finish the work of revolution and change the world to a place where all could thrive and live free.

Louis Auguste Blanqui had been trying to lead new revolutions and return France to a republic since he had been my age in the 1830s. Thanks to those indiscretions, he had spent most of his life in prison for his radical ideals, but that had not stopped his idea from spreading or prevented him from gaining followers.

In the summer of 1870, his men were organized and implanted throughout Paris. They worked in cells of no more than ten men each, preparing, organizing, and – most importantly – arming for the day they knew would come soon. The day when the people would rise up again.

Though I had never taken up arms for any cause before, it felt inevitable to join the Blanquists when I was finally introduced to a cell. They were led by a man named Laurent. He was barely a few years older than me, but he burned with a sort of divine fire of conviction that warmed and compelled every person around him.

Laurent was ready to light a blaze that would not only burn down the Emperor, but the very world that allowed empires and nobility to even exist. In a cellar below a cheese shop, he rallied his band of soldiers. He looked me in the eyes without suspicion or fear and said that in the new world we would build, there would be no masks, no need for anyone, however they were made by God, to hide their face. He was the sort of man that when he spoke you had no choice but to believe him. And I did. I fell a bit in love that night and I signed on with no hesitation to serve the cause.

I was just in time.

It was late June when I swore myself to Laurent and the Blanquists. By July, France was a powder keg, and it was a telegram, of all things, that set the spark. Bismarck shared a dispatch with the press: an edited account of the King of Prussia offhandedly dismissing France's demands regarding the Spanish succession and never allowing a German to take that throne. It sounds quite silly, doesn't it? All these machinations of generals and kings and how they can lead to the loss of lives and empires. But the French were hungry for war and took the German insult as exactly the bait Bismarck intended.

I was there in our cellar below the cheese shop (which always smelled of Roquefort and thus was rarely explored by sensible people) when a young man ran in with the news of the so-called "Ems Dispatch" and how it had set the people off. There were thousands marching in the streets, calling for war. Most of the cell joined them, but Laurent and I stayed. He looked at me and said he could tell I was a fighter, that I had seen blood and danger. He wanted to know what preparations we still needed to make for the coming conflagration.

"We will need to find a base with more room than a cheese shop," I said, half-joking.

"Where would you have us go?"

I didn't answer immediately. Rather I had him follow me up onto the roof of the building, three stories up where we could see the crowds streaming down the wide *Avenue de l'Opéra* to the newly minted heart of the city where five different streets met and spread out like spokes on a wheel. At that grand crossroad stood a glorious, huge, empty building, ready to be filled with soldiers, supplies, and more.

"Napoleon III built himself that Opera after an anarchist tried to kill him at the old one," I explained. "But music belongs to the people, not the kings. I think we should steal his dearest jewel while he's off playing at war."

"I knew there was a reason we chose you, Erik."

That night I led our cell through the tunnels of Paris to the unfinished Palais Garnier. I expected to feel the way I always did breaking into a theater or manor when I stepped into the unfinished Opera, but there was no sense of alienness or anxiety there. For the first time, I stepped into a darkened building in secret, and it felt like coming home. Maybe it was fate, or the spirit of the place itself knew I was tied to her story. Whatever the reason, I resolved that night to stay at the Opera as much as I could. That would not be easy though.

The telegram and subsequent uprising in the city arrived on July 13th and by the 16th, France was formally at war. The Emperor rushed off to join his armies and the troops mustered. In Paris, men everywhere were called into service of the National Guard just as the Blanquists and other communards had hoped. Throughout the Guard, we had been placed in positions of power and control. We were ready for when it was time to strike. I was not among them, of course, I had other preparations to make.

I had won my audience with the Blanquists by telling the right person that I had useful skills, including those of a builder. It wasn't a lie. I'd loved and studied architecture since Florence, and among the few honest means of making a living I'd undertaken over the years, masonry and construction had been my favorite. It felt good to create something that would last, even if no one would ever know. Yet in my heart, I remained a magician who lived life hidden in shadows and masks. Why not combine two passions, then?

Construction on the Opera slowed and eventually halted as the war escalated, and we took great advantage of the opportunity to have our way with the unfinished building I envisioned as our new base. I became a new architect of the Opera at night, building sliding walls and installing trap doors. I added a hollow column to a box on the grand tier, thinking of how easy it would be to attend with such a secret entrance. I installed secret tunnels throughout late summer while the armies skirmished to the east.

The Prussians were winning, the papers said. They had marshalled their forces faster and were advancing quickly into France. Too quickly for the Emperor to hold back. He was losing ground in the countryside, unaware that he was also losing Paris to the people he had abandoned.

I had such ideals then that I cringe to remember myself, but I think many feel the same way when they have the privilege of looking back at twenty-five with a decade's distance. We filled the Opera's empty cellars with weapons as the National Guard filled her unfinished halls and rehearsal rooms with supplies and grain (safety measure for if the Prussians were to reach the city). Surely, we thought, that would not happen. We'd win our revolution first, and I was ready for it. When the people took back the country, it would be a place *I* could live in as a man without fear. Laurent made me believe that, and I convinced everyone I met of the same thing. For a few weeks, it seemed like it would happen.

At the beginning of September, word reached the city that the Emperor had been defeated and captured at the battle of Sedan, and finally the spark was lit. The workers of France and Paris rose up, and within two days the Second Empire was dead and the Third Republic was declared. It had begun. The world was about to be rewritten and we would be its authors.

That night we celebrated. Or everyone else did. I watched, quietly (and nervously) from corners as the festivities went on, watched my brothers in arms take whores up to the rooms, above the cheese shop that had been transformed into a makeshift tavern for the night.

Laurent was careful not to show favoritism to anyone – except for his women. Some of the women that joined us were as radical as we were, and some were there to fuck for gold, but the best of both always went to Laurent's rooms. Laurent insisted on paying all of them, even though I think they would have gone to his bed for free. He said they deserved their coins. Even his favorite, Mireille.

Mireille was beautiful in the way a monastery fallen to ruin and overgrown with weeds can be beautiful. There was something visible in her underfed frame and rouged cheeks of the coquette she had been years before. By the time of the revolution, her skin was washed out and spent, but she still drew men to her bed for a coin. It was Laurent she served the most, but that night, I felt as giddy as my comrades with the start of our new world and I considered drinking myself into bravery and going to her.

It had been a long time since I had allowed myself anything more than superficial pleasure when it came to lust. I could attend to my body's demands, arouse and release myself as needed; but since that bloody night in Venice, I had never thought to go to another lover's bed. I knew I could have done it, paid a whore of any sort to take me to bed. I even could have found release in a well-paid mouth in an alley if I had wanted it, but I never wanted it. Any time I had even come close to attempting such a transaction my skin had tightened and my stomach had turned in panic. I had no need for touch. Indeed, I rather feared it.

But among the communards, intoxicated with the dream of a future where I could truly be among people, I considered it. But Laurent got to her first and led her upstairs. I found myself listening to their performance just as I had listened in guilt and lust to Constance and Steiner years before. It was pain, jealousy, and longing I felt more than lust. I don't know which of them I envied more.

I listened to Mireille's theatrical moans as Laurent grunted and groaned and I wondered what they both felt like. Did she feel warm close to his fire, bathed in the holy light of conviction that shone from him? Did he feel something like love in her embrace? Or was it just release? It was so strange to think of just enjoying pleasure when I knew so much pain. I pictured them in the throes of passion and cringed at the thought of myself in their place.

I ran off into the night before they finished, the loneliness I had run from for so long choking me. I ran to the Opera, the unfinished behemoth that had been such a comfort in the last month, and I descended downward into the depths and to the places even the brave revolutionaries had been frightened to go. I wasn't frightened that night. I wanted to be as far from humanity as possible by my own choice, not because of some curse.

So it was that night, as Paris revolted and reveled above me, that I first came to the lake. To call it a lake was perhaps a bit of poetic license. I had read in Garnier's revised plans for the Opera (which I had liberated from a government office weeks before) about the great cistern he had been forced to install in the foundations to hold the water from an underground stream and keep the site from sinking into a bog. It was beautiful, with its columns and arches rising from still, cold water. It smelled like cobblestones and dry earth after rain, an eternal note of petrichor in the dark air.

I skirted the edge of the lagoon, examining the double casing for openings or places to make them. I found two. One was near the mouth path from behind the stage, more convenient one might say. The space between the first wall keeping the water in and the outer layer was dark and cavernous, like a tomb, and I shivered to think what might be done there.

The second opening was much smaller; perfect, I thought, for a door that would conceal a hidden space. I considered sleeping there that very night, but it was already dawn above by the time I had finished exploring. For the next two weeks, I went down to the lake each night. In my mind I named it after a lake I had visited once in Italy, that the Romans had believed was the entrance to the underworld: Lake Avernus.

By the end of a fortnight, I had created a rather comfortable little lakeside getaway for myself. It was safe and hidden, stocked with food and candles and books. Preparing my hiding place would prove to be one of the smartest things I had ever done, because in mid-September the Prussian Army arrived on Paris's doorstep. The siege of Paris had begun.

The new republican government set up in Versailles did not end the war. They did nothing when the Prussians barricaded the roads, shelled the city, and placed Paris under siege. The greatest city in the world would not fall and certainly, now that the Emperor was gone, the new leadership would be able to do what he could not and break the will of the German war machine.

Days passed, then weeks. September faded into October. The nights grew longer and colder. Then the food started to run out. A city runs on bread and meat, and when the bread and meat stop coming in from the country, the city starves. The only news or correspondence came from air mail dropped by balloons, but no one cared. Our bellies were growling and the people were becoming wild and ravenous. I had never needed much sustenance to survive, but I began to worry how much more like a skeleton I would soon look.

They started to eat the horses by the end of November. Then the cats and dogs and rats. In our cell, Laurent ordered that we were to keep our diets to bread and meager stews – let the people have the meat. I think he wanted a reason to not consume someone's treasured pet and I fully supported it. I discovered to my delight that my lake had a few fish, but they were devilishly hard to catch.

We worked for the people, we told ourselves. We protected them and were readying the city for the greater changes that would come when the siege was broken. But there was little for bored revolutionaries to do. The men were hungry, ready for a fight that refused to come, and tired of decades of inaction and world only getting worse while the politicians and oligarchs did nothing to protect the people. We couldn't even protect the people from their empty bellies and the coldest winter in memory. Men with nothing to fight and hate in their hearts are good at creating enemies. So that's what they did.

It was Laurent who hauled the man into headquarters (now located in the main floor of the cheese shop, since all the product had been eaten months before) and presented him, bloody and beaten. He was trying to undo the revolution, we were told. He wanted to restore the Emperor and welcome the Germans into the city. He had confessed as much under Laurent's fists. He had to be brought to justice.

There was no need for a jury, and justice was too slow, just like the endless and useless committees that debated all day throughout the city and did nothing. This would be justice by the people. We would end this threat and eradicate it, Laurent cried, his conviction and passion so unquestionable you could feel it course through the room. We all jumped though, even me, when he pulled out his pistol and shot the spy in the head.

We should have stopped right there. We should have said it had all gone too far and dispersed immediately. But we didn't. Someone cheered, and I think it was then, not months later when the men in that room lay dead in the streets or hung from the rafters of that room, that our revolution really died.

Laurent came to me the next day. He had always liked talking to me, or so it seemed, and I confess the thrill it gave me when he looked at me, not only without fear, but like I was the only person worth seeing. I had told him of my adventures and misadventures, how I had learned the cruelty of men and nobility. Didn't I want to finally strike back? Didn't I want to save this country? I could do it by helping him. By finding the spies. I said yes without hesitation. I was young and stupid and in love with him and all the delusions and dreams he embodied.

When the empire fell in September, we had been idealists. But in the depths of winter, we became madmen. As the rich dined on Christmas menus that included the elephants from the zoo in the *Bois de Boulogne*, cells like ours turned on what we thought was the real threat: fellow men who might compromise our ideals. I helped them. I hurt people and it felt righteous and good. When those men refused to reveal who they were sending information to, I knew where to put them.

I'd found the mirrors in a half-finished salon in the Opera above, and my comrades had gleefully helped me move them to my hiding places by the lake. We started keeping prisoners in the large room, but next to my smaller abode we built the most fiendish thing I could conceive: a torture chamber like Steiner's but worse. I made it back into a carnival amusement with the use of lime lights and painted corners. I created a devilish forest for our prisoners that could drive them mad in a matter of hours. We only used it for those who refused to break, but Laurent found it delightful. I was so happy to have made him proud.

The siege ended in January, as I found myself turning twenty-six (or so I estimated), and once again we were filled with hope. The winter winds still blew cold as the city struggled back to her feet. With the end of the siege came the loss of the war. The Third Republic had begun its life with failure, and the people would not stand it when they tried to take our arms and cannons back.

By March, Paris had healed and the people were ready to rise. The siege of Paris was over, but we took to the streets and declared that a new era was beginning, the era of the Paris Commune. It would be as the revolutionaries had truly envisioned it when they cut off Louis's head. Some were quite serious about this and forced a return to the ludicrous revolutionary calendar that no one understood. That was a trifle compared to the return of the infamous "committee for public safety." Such a strange name for a group of bloodthirsty anarchists ready for a new reign of terror.

The sun was returning, it was spring, but it felt like every day grew darker as the Commune reigned. Laurent's little battalion had swelled in size, and the Opera officially became our barracks and armory. It was perfect now, full of secret passages I had built and packed with arms and gun powder. Her darkest and most useful function, however, was holding prisoners and we had so many. Everywhere we turned it seemed was a new traitor.

The ones who ended up in the bowels of the Opera, locked away beside the lake, were the lucky ones. Half the enemies of the people caught by the Commune ended up dead before they could be shut away. The whole city had gone mad and by May, there was no pretending we were fighting for ideals. I was caught up in my tortures at Laurent's behest and realized too late the monsters we had become. Or always had been.

The army – the real army, not the National Guard that had taken the city as part of the Commune – arrived on the 22$^{nd}$ of May. It began what they would call "Bloody Week" in the histories. It was a slaughter. Barricades rose in the streets, the fighting was everywhere, and it was immediately clear that we were going to all die if we stayed. I fled the sound of gunfire and marching troops back down to the Opera cellars to warn Laurent. He had been there constantly for weeks, and I had been forced to give up my quiet little home to make room for a project he promised would amaze me.

I found the prisoners first. He had killed them before they could be freed by the republicans and before they could see Laurent's great plan. He had moved barrels and barrels of gun powder into my chambers beside the lake and he was ready, he said, to light the spark at last. When the republicans arrived at the Opera above to take our arms, we would destroy them and this imperialist monument to the bourgeois. It would hop like a grasshopper, he raved; so much gun powder would blow the entire building to dust! With that righteous, beautiful fire in his eyes he went on and on. We would die birthing the new world that would rise from the rubble! Would I join him in striking the match?

The Punjab lasso claimed his life before he could take up his torch. He fell like a stone, the light finally extinguished from his heroic face. I wept then, kneeling by his side. I wept for the dreams that had been lies, and the dreams of a future that would never come true. I wept for my own stupidity in believing that anything in the world could change. I wept for my friend and carried his body to lie with the other prisoners. And I left the Opera, the first place I had ever felt at home, for what I thought was the last time.

I found myself back at our old headquarters, where the few of us who didn't want to die at the army's hands had taken refuge. Mireille was there, as beautiful and faded as before, and ever the optimist, she was open for business. I was utterly alone, I realized. I always had been. Why not take some goddamn cold comfort before my judgement arrived with the republican troops?

She took me to a room upstairs, I don't know whose it was. She was merciful and kind. She let me blow out the candles, so that the only light came from the fires burning in the street below. She knew I was afraid and that I was as inept as any virgin. She used her hands on my cock to get me hard and said pretty things about how much she liked it, how good it would feel in her. She could have been a great actress, that woman. Then she stripped off her clothes like it was nothing, climbed on the bed, and went onto her hands and knees. She'd usually make her customers wear a prophylactic of some sort, a contraption of sheep guts, but what was the point tonight?

It felt mechanical, the way it happened. No fumbling rush like in Venice. Just a transaction that made part of my tired body feel good and warm. She made the same noises for me she'd made for Laurent as my cock did its work. When I came, it was dull and quick, and I felt just as numb after as when I'd started. She laughed when I paid her double the usual price, wondering where I found the money. I didn't stay. I went into back out and tried to stay alive.

I went to a cemetery and hid in a crypt, the living dead among the real corpses. It was the safest place and I would survive there. I deserved death, everyone who had been part of that bloody delusion did. But since birth the one constant in my miserable life had been just that – life. I refused to let go of it, even in the worst moments.

I refused to give into death. He had marked me since birth, and I would defy him out of pure spite for as long as I could. So I hid for days as the streets flowed with blood and piled up with bodies beside the barricades. When the gunshots stopped, I went back to see who of my so-called comrades had lived. All of them were hanging from the rafters of the shop with Mireille beside them. She was the only one I cut down and buried as well as I could, back in the crypt that had saved me, the only one for whom I sang a requiem.

I made my way to the coast and stowed away on a boat bound north, I didn't care where. I wanted to be done with Prussia and France and Britain and their wars and empires and republics. It was all the same thing, all different versions of a world that was broken and had no place in it for me. I was done fighting kings and hoping for a new world.

So two years later, when I found myself the talk of the Great Fair of Nizhny Novgorod and a man claiming to work for the Shah of Persia offered me a place in a royal court, I savored the irony of accepting. Maybe I had been doing things wrong all along. Perhaps if I served a royal, I would find the glory and joy I deserved.

My dreams were to be mistaken once again.

# 6. Danse de Perse

*"You're still a rebel and a radical at heart, you know."*
*"I am. But it's an impulse I have better understanding of and control over now, after a decade of disillusionment."*
*"Did serving a royal change your perspective back?"*
*"Serving the Shah changed the way I saw everything."*
*"Was it the Shah? Or was it him?"*

I hadn't meant to stay in Russia as long as I did, but the Russian winter had defeated me just as it had Napoleon, and a journey back to the west through the blizzard did not appeal to me. I was already missing a nose – no need to tempt fate and let frostbite take any other appendage. I didn't like Russia particularly. Her music was so deep and dark and the dispositions of her people were just as gloomy. I could understand it, I guess, given what their Tsar put them through. After seeing the failure of the Commune, I was quite disillusioned with the idea that anything anywhere could change for the better without a bloodbath.

It was not such a dreadful thing to linger there. The Great Fair at Nizhny Novgorod on the shores of the Volga was a perfect refuge. Audiences and their money came to me, and I returned with delight to my pursuits in illusion, ventriloquism, and music. The crowds came from all around, and soon my reputation spread through the caravan and trade routes. All the way to the court of Naser al-Din Shah Qajar of Persia. He sent one of his more trusted constables (and best spies) to find me and bring me back as a new treasure for his glorious court.

Shaya Motlagh was in his thirties when I first met him. I saw all sorts of people at the Great Fair, but even among the crowds, he stood out when he first attended my performance. Olive skinned with a neatly trimmed beard, he had deep brown eyes that were always sharp, always looking for something more. Shaya wore his Astrakhan hat like a badge of honor, proud for everyone that saw him to know he came from the greatest civilization on the earth. When he approached me, after the rest of the crowds had left, I first guessed that he wanted to know the secret to some illusion. He said he would rather discover the truth himself first.

He made his offer instead, and I laughed in his face. I had no interest in his Shah, no matter how grand his royal residence or how much he could pay me. I had never been swayed by money because any money I'd ever needed, I'd simply taken. Shaya saw that immediately and offered me something better: glory and adventure in a new land on the cusp of joining the great powers once again.

He spoke with utter love when it came to his country and deep devotion when it came to Naser al-Din. This Shah was no tyrant, he claimed; he was a modern monarch determined to bring his country into the continental world. I supported the Shah's desire to show Britain and France and the Ottomans that Persia was still as great as it had been under Cyrus, Darius, and Xerxes.

I was fascinated. I had missed Persia entirely on my first journey to the East, but it always intrigued me. Despite falling under the control of so many empires over the centuries, Persia had remained itself; a beacon of learning and art throughout the world, and this Shah hoped to make her such a jewel again. He was even building a new modern palace in the coast country. Shaya said he knew the architect and I would love it.

I went with him, intoxicated by the dream of something new (and happy to be going somewhere warm and leaving the Russian chill behind me). I had to convince myself to go, tell myself that maybe *this* was the chance I had been seeking for a decade to be more than a carnival freak or an outcast. I could have influence in a great court. I could build something that would last if, I played things right. I should have listened to my instincts.

I was not prepared for the beauty of Persia when I arrived. It reminded me of Rome or Athens, a city in a country that had history going back millennia, but here it was alive and honored and not in ruins. I stepped into a tapestry of stories woven over centuries, of peoples and traditions that were familiar and strange at the same time. Shaya was so happy to be my guide, for he took such pride in his Iran.

The people of that land did not call it "Persia." That is the foreigner's way of referring to it, all the way back to their wars with the Greeks of Sparta and Athens. For them, it has always been "Iran." Persian is the language, and even that is a European bastardization of "Farsi." Shaya was sure to tell me all of this and more as we traveled the country.

Wearing a mask all one's life, all around the world, leads one to unique experiences and skills. I always know as soon as I reach a new place how long I might stay or what kind of reception I will have, depending on how they look at a man who covers his face. Over my travels, I had adopted a variety of masks, some more theatrical than others, of varied materials, textures, and shapes. Some covered my mouth, others didn't. When performing, I liked my lips to be seen, to create more wonder when I spoke or sang without moving them. But when traveling in distant lands, I liked to cover my face entirely, so as not to mark myself as an outsider in multiple ways.

That was how I arrived in Tehran, the great capital, with a dark mask over my whole face. I noted the way people peered at me from market stalls as I rode by. There was more fascination than fear, and I began to foolishly feel something like hope. Maybe this place was more enlightened, like Shaya said. Maybe I wouldn't be a monster.

We arrived at the palace in the evening, and I was shown to rooms far finer than anything I had enjoyed before in my life on the road. There was so much space here to fill with books and trinkets, and I quite liked it. The building itself was particularly beautiful. I told Shaya as much when he came to inform me of our plans. That pleased him because he had returned in the company of the building's architect: his brother.

His name was Ramin. He was younger than Shaya and his opposite in so many ways. Shaya was a man of tradition who saw what his country could accomplish and be if the world were to recognize the greatness she already possessed. Ramin had hope for what she could be with the right guides and looked to the future and the West with excitement and interest. He wore fewer traditional clothes, he kept himself clean-shaven, and his handsomeness was soft and inviting, like a warm summer evening's light, whereas Shaya was sharp as a cold breeze off the sea.

Shaya informed me that I was to be introduced to the Shah and his entire court at a party thrown in my "honor" where I was to entertain. But that would not happen for two nights and until then I could rest and make myself at home. I wasn't sure what to do with all that time and I think Ramin sensed that, so he immediately invited me to dine and engaged me in conversation.

Shaya, I had learned, was a man of facts and hard truths. He had to be in his work for the Shah, which he was quite mysterious about explaining. The world was black and white to him. The will of Allah and the words of the Prophet were truth, and the service of the Shah and his country were the highest calling. But Ramin... He was a poet. He saw the world in a thousand colors and I liked the world much better through his eyes.

He was full of endless questions, Ramin, about me and all the places I had been and what I had seen. I'm surprised he talked with me at all. I was jaded and sarcastic and generally as insufferable as a young man of twenty-seven who thought he knew everything could be. Ramin seemed a man of the world, unfettered by tradition and dogma, and I could not understand why he was wasting his time in the same place he had spent his whole life when there was a world to see. He told me simply that this was his home and he loved it.

I laughed, like the pompous ass I was. Love – of country or anything else – was a drug and a delusion. I thought I was so smart.

*"Eshg hich vaght gonah nist,"* he had said. My Farsi was poor at the time (whereas Shaya and Ramin's French was immaculate). I didn't know then what he meant, but the way he said it, a bit sad and wistful, made me want to learn.

By the time I was set to appear before the Shah and his court I was not nervous because I wanted to impress a gaggle of nobility. I wanted to impress Ramin and earn the right to stay in the place he and Shaya had made seem so beautiful.

The audience was only men I noticed immediately when I arrived and took my place on the dais that had been set up for me. I would learn later that in the balcony above, the women were watching too, unseen behind a screen. It was uncouth for men to look upon women who belonged to the Shah, but not for said Shah to fill his court with foreigners who ogled Persia herself like lechers. Of course it was the British who had wormed their way into another court, perhaps hoping to steal away Persia from the Shah like they had taken India from the Raj. It was no matter who was watching. I was prepared to dazzle, and so I did. For an hour, I filled their eyes with wonders and their ears with haunting song.

At the end, as always, came the moment – the moment I hated. The Shah himself demanded I remove my mask. I was defiant, as always, loathe to do as ordered even when I knew in my heart it needed to be done.

There sat the Shah, in his military regalia, his court of toadies and spies holding their breath all around us. He spoke perfect French, like the modern European monarch he wanted to be. In the corner were Shaya and Ramin. Shaya had already seen my face at my performance in Russia. Surely, he had told his younger brother of the horror. And if that was the case, I only had to confirm what I was. And why did I care anyway?

I pulled off the mask with a flourish and presented myself in all my morbid glory to the mighty court. There was not a sound in the great hall. No one let their faces betray an ounce of terror until the Shah reacted first. For an agonizing minute, we waited. Then, the Shah applauded and laughed.

No one screamed. They tittered politely, and I put my mask back on.

"I should like to keep you, Erik," the Shah said and the deal was done.

I stayed, one of many foreigners and magicians in the employ of a man who only hated one thing more than boredom: betrayal. But I didn't know that yet. I didn't know that he laughed at the horrors of my face because horror was something he quite enjoyed.

The Shah was not the only one I was to entertain. After a few days, I was brought to amuse the women. The Shah's harem was kept sequestered, along with his mother and the widows of the former Shah. I felt a sort of sympathy for them: being locked away thanks to how they were born, seen as only useful for the amusements their bodies could provide. The Shah kept huge golden cages filled with parrots, doves, and all sorts of exotic songbirds, and it felt no different from the way he treated those women.

At least they were not alone in their captivity, I told myself. They were attended by eunuchs and had one another. I said as much to

Ramin, and he happily remedied me of that optimistic view. The harem was as competitive and cutthroat as the court. The women pitted themselves against one another for favor with their husband and preference for their children, and those fights could be deadly.

Still, I took more pleasure in amusing them than I did the Shah. I would sing or play outside their veiled windows in the courtyard, as close as I was permitted to them, and I'd watch their silhouettes as they leaned against the walls and listened to my voice and looked up to the sliver of sky they were permitted to see. Were they like me in my prison in Vienna or my mother's home, hidden away because of how they were born and condemned to be used? Were they dreaming of the wide world? I sang them sad songs so that maybe they would realize that the wide world was just as full of pain.

It was a curious thing to be a court entertainer. I had no use for politics anymore and I hated people, so I was useless with intrigues, but I still found myself at the center of them. It's always dangerous to be the smartest man in the room, and to remind others of that fact. I was skilled in many fields, and at first, men of the court came to consult me. Then they came to consult me about the other men who had consulted me. And then some of them became threatened by my mere existence. Even though I wanted nothing that they had, they saw an outsider with skills and intelligence greater than theirs and were sure I was about to take what was theirs because that was what people did.

I learned quickly that the court was full of spies, and that everyone of influence had their own little networks. All those people seemed to be working at cross purposes. This one wanted advancement for his family, that one wanted a contract for such and such business, this diplomat wanted favorable trade while another wanted a monopoly. The clerics wanted one thing, while the scientists wanted another. At the center was the Shah, being pulled and manipulated in all directions.

For years, Naser Al-Din had tried to modernize and change Iran, but he kept failing, kept falling behind. He had tried to force the country to emulate the West, to be like England or France, but Iran was already itself; it could not become a pale copy of a lesser civilization, according to the people. They resisted his every attempt to wipe away the old and traditional and replace it with the new. In some ways, I cannot blame him for the paranoid and cruel man he had become. He was jaded and sure that everyone around him was there only to use him. The tragedy was that he was not entirely wrong.

Naser Al-Din had the greatest network of spies and detectives in the entire court, and his best *Daroga* was Shaya, I discovered. He trusted him to watch all of those who he kept as amusements, as well as his women and his enemies. But I didn't mind Shaya spying on me, because that meant he invited me to dine often with him and his brother, and there was no one in the court whose company I enjoyed more than Ramin's.

He had given me a gift, you see. The night after I had shown my face and met him in the courtyard, where the air was heavy with the scent of roses, I had waited for his comment or for his eyes to change. All he had said was: "It's really not as bad as I had been led to believe." And that was the end of it. I knew it was a lie, of course, but it was the kindest lie anyone had ever told me.

T hey were a strange pair, the brothers Motlagh. Both unmarried and yet holding high positions in court, they had noble ancestry. Their influential extended family granted them certain privileges and a sizable estate, but they were small in comparison to the giants that circled the Shah. That was why they were both useful to him. Shaya was not so well-known that he couldn't move undetected, and Ramin was not so famous that he cost too much to employ in Naser Al-Din's quests to build great monuments to show off his power.

It did not take me long to learn from Ramin why Shaya was not married. He told me his brother's secrets with loving amusement: Shaya had no wife or lover or anyone else because he did not feel the need. He enjoyed the companionship of family and friends, and there was no one he trusted more in the world outside his kin than his servant, Darius. But Shaya felt no desire for flesh or fucking and found the way lust muddled people's minds and ruined lives quite perplexing. Ramin had been the one, he told me, to convince Shaya that this was not some failure in his making, but a blessing. He was unattached and unaffected by that which brought so many men low and could doom so many others.

Ramin had looked so sad when he said that, as if his own lust were a burden, and I guessed there was some lover in his past that had broken his heart. I was not entirely wrong, but I would not learn that for a while yet. My time with the brothers was the highlight of those first months. Ramin enjoyed needling his conservative older brother, shocking him with some new idea or blasphemy, and I enjoyed interloping into a truly loving family when I found my way to their apartments. It was Ramin who helped me practice my Farsi, who loaned me his copies of the poems of Rumi, Saadi, Khayyam, and Attar of Nishapur's *The Conference of the Birds*.

Ramin was a Muslim in outward practice, but he also studied the teachings of Zoroaster, and I listened with great interest as he relayed to me ancient tales of the battle between light and dark, as that same light from a sacred fire danced upon his face.

He wanted to hear my stories too, and final, after much prying, I shared them. There was something about him that made me feel as if I could share anything, as if he could look at the ugliness and simply smile. He learned of my love of architecture and immediately began consulting me on his designs for the Shah's new pleasure palace set to be built in the resort province of Mazenderan, by the Caspian Sea where the relentless heat of Tehran never reached.

I had never had such a friend, and with Shaya on the periphery, I felt as if I had two. I feared what he would think of my past, but I trusted him, so finally, one dark night, he learned of the bloodshed I had caused. He did not judge. He absolved me. Or tried to. He said I was more than my crimes.

Shaya seemed to disagree. He looked at me differently after his brother shared the truth with him. I had not sworn him to secrecy. I did not want to make him lie to his brother. I knew what I was. I was still damned, even if Ramin disagreed.

After several months in Tehran, the Shah began to tire of me. I would not have minded being sent off on more wanderings, had I not become so attached to my place there and the people. I had a home there, or the beginnings of it, finally. I had felt as if I had finally laid the foundations of a future. I could never be a normal man, but in Persia, I did not need to be. I could see myself there for years, watching as the edifice of a new life rose, like Ramin's palace at Mazenderan that I had already begun to think of partly as my creation.

Shaya had decided it was time for me to move on as well. He knew my secrets and he, keen-eyed and perceptive as ever, knew I was cursed and that it would not be long before that curse claimed his little brother. He wanted to protect his family, so he made his move. He told the Shah that I was a killer. Suddenly, I was not so boring to the monarch.

It was in the Mazenderan palace, half-completed and already sumptuous and entrancing, that I was called on to perform in a new way for the Shah. I was led into a courtyard, stripped down to shirtsleeves, and unmasked. I looked unarmed, but the Punjab lasso was wrapped around my waist, ready as always. That was what the Shah was hoping to see.

"I have heard, Erik the Magician, that you have a unique skill. You can kill a man with a rope and nothing more, like the legendary stranglers of India," Nasr Al-Din said from on high in a balcony, Shaya hiding at his elbow, a look of remorse and terror in his face. "Show us."

The door opposite me opened and out of it strode a man armed with a pike and knife. I recognized him and so did Shaya. He had spoken against the Shah weeks before, so Shaya and the secret police had come for him in the night. He was a traitor condemned to die – unless he earned freedom in exile by killing me. If I killed him, I could keep my life.

It was precious to me, my life. It was the one thing no one could take away. My breath which gave me music, my heartbeat which fed my dreams. I would not die like that, in the dirt at a nobles' whim. I would not give my fate to them. I would give them my curse instead. When I strangled that man with my Punjab Lasso, the court applauded as if it was a new magic trick. I was glad Ramin wasn't there to see.

With a flick of that lasso, the dream I could be anything more than a monster, died again. From then on, I was the Shah's favorite executioner, and my displays of skill in ending a life were as well-attended and adored as my performances of magic and music. My will was law, and everyone feared me. Everyone except the Shah, who wielded me like a weapon, and Shaya and Ramin, who knew my humanity. But one of them had already begun to turn thanks to his Shah.

There was rot in the court of the Shah, I saw that clearly once I was free from my illusions of a new life there. It was like a perfect fruit that was being eaten from the inside by magots and the Shah was the worm at the center of it all. This cruel, paranoid man had been a reformer in his youth. Just like me, he had dreamed of change and been filled with hope, only to find that the world had no use for such delusions, especially the powerful of Europe whom he had invited into his court. He had been the frog of the old parable, trusting a scorpion not to sting him. But men in power cannot help their nature. They are all scorpions and they all stung again and again until Naser Al-Din's beloved country was on its knees.

By the time I came to his court, Naser al-Din had already become the weakest kind of ruler. He cared only for keeping power and using it for his own pleasure, no matter how his people suffered. I did not realize it for months, thanks to the wealth of the court at which I enjoyed myself, but I had come to Persia in the midst of a terrible famine. While the Shah threw banquets and emptied his country's coffers to build his jewel box palace at Mazenderan, thousands starved, and the Shah didn't care. He saw it as their failure, for not listening to him. He had Shaya and the rest of his secret police track down anyone who questioned him. I gave those dissidents death.

When I couldn't sleep because of the nightmares, I told myself I was the instrument. I was the gun he fired at his enemies. *I* wasn't the one who chose their moment to return to Allah. It was him. It was all him and I had no choice or control. The lie gave me some comfort in those rosy hours of Mazenderan.

Shaya knew what his master was capable of, but it began to be me he feared and looked upon with disgust. Or so I thought. Ramin refused to give up on me and held onto me all the more tightly as those months went on. Ramin always wanted me with him, because if I was with him, I was safe, and so was everyone else.

"You are an artist Erik – the most sublime I have ever known. You must see that," he told me one night. "You cannot waste your gifts on death."

"Death is the only gift this world will allow me to bestow. She has turned away all my other offers," I shot back.

"Not everyone. Not all of us."

I didn't listen to his entreaties. Instead, I turned to helping him with the palace as much as I could. Yet that too became corrupted because the Shah had learned another horror of my past.

I was to do on purpose what I had done piecemeal with the Commune: design a mystery box, where the Shah could move about unseen to do his own spying upon all that would defy him. He was suspicious of his women especially. Their rooms would be lined with mirrors that were windows to him, and he would be able to observe all their sins and secrets. That was his idea, but mine was to create the most terrible place once again I had ever been, a maze of mirrors that would drive men mad. A new torture chamber.

Ramin saw it as a betrayal, to have such an abomination inserted into his beautiful work. I told him that he was building a palace for the real abomination. He worked for a man who killed those that defied him and who infected his whole land – the land Ramin loved so – with malice and hate. Whether I was there or not, it didn't matter, the result would be the same.

"What if we fought back, then?" Ramin asked aloud at last. "What if we did something?"

But it was too late. By the time Ramin confronted me, it was already done. The palace was nearly completed. Soon dozens, hundreds even, would enter its walls, and the Shah – the law and leader himself – would make sure they never escaped if he suspected them of betrayal. Ramin said we could warn them. We could alert the diplomats, tell the people. Shaya was a good man; he would help us if we asked!

I called Ramin an idealist and a fool but he went to his brother anyway. Of course, Shaya knew the Shah's plans and had his own orders. The Shah suspected I would reveal his palace's secrets and he had grown bored with me again. This time, my death was assured. Shaya would be the one to do it.

Ramin, to say the least, objected. He railed against his brother, asking him what had become of his soul, and Shaya seized him. He was doing this *for* Ramin. If Shaya killed me, the Shah had agreed to let Ramin live. Shaya had no choice but to end the life of the man he had called a friend! It was for the best anyway, he told his brother. I was a corrupting influence and it was high time for Ramin's infatuation with the infidel magician with the face of a devil and the voice of an angel to end.

All of this Ramin told me as soon as he could. He rushed into my quarters, warning me that the Daroga of Mazenderan was on his way with his two most trusted deputies. I was in shock, not because of the death sentence – that made perfect sense if the Shah wanted to keep his secrets. What I did not understand was why Ramin wanted to save me, and why Shaya wanted to keep his brother from my side. What spell had I cast that I did not recall?

Ramin smiled. He had the most wonderful smile – it had always made me feel so normal and so welcome. But that night, as the oil lamps burned and the crickets sang outside my window, he smiled at me like I was the sweetest fool he had ever encountered. "You know so much, Erik. But my brother, he's the one who sees. He saw months ago that I had become a fool for love when it came to you. Don't you understand?"

I didn't. I couldn't. But I ran with him anyway.

I should have told him to stay and let me escape. I should have told him he was a fool indeed for thinking I could be saved or that I deserved his mercy or his heart. But I didn't. I ran with him and condemned us all.

In the years since, I have forced myself to imagine what Shaya experienced when he found us both gone. Did he know then that his brother was good as dead? Did he still hope to save us? The Shah's reaction was much easier to guess. Shaya had broken their deal, so Ramin was marked for death. Shaya's life was now at stake, and the Shah gave him the choice to prove his loyalty and save himself. But Shaya was not me and he would not shed any blood to save his life. He refused to hunt Ramin down, so he too was condemned.

It was Darius who freed Shaya and allowed him to escape, joining his master in exile and damnation. He took Shaya to a safe house, then went to arrange passage for Shaya, and hopefully Ramin, to somewhere they could flee safely. But Shaya had to find us first.

It was all too easy and that was the point. They let Darius free his master, and when Shaya went to hunt us down, they followed him. The Shah knew no one would be better suited to finding Ramin than his own brother. And he knew I would be a fool and be found with him.

We had found ourselves in a little house by the Caspian, where the breeze was cool and everything was green. It was beautiful. It had belonged to some cousin or friend of his, I think. He was not devious, Ramin; he didn't realize a familiar place was one of the first Shaya would look for us. But we had a few days' head start at least and we weren't going to stay long.

"We can go. We can leave. We can go *together*." I still remember how sure he seemed when he said those words and how I laughed. Why would he ask such a thing or believe it was possible? Why would he leave his land for me of all people?

The same reason, he told me, that he had stayed for so long. For love. Was it not clear?

"Love?" I asked back, in mockery because it was such an absurd idea.

"It's not impossible, Erik, for someone to care for you as you are," he replied, cowed and shy for the first time.

"How can you say that though? Is it not an abomination in your faith, for you to love a man – not to mention a monster? Why would you give in to such sin?"

I will never forget the way he looked at me, the peace and light in his eyes when he shook his head. "I have known what I am since I was young. My brother has tried with all his might to protect me, though not to understand. I have been left to that quest alone. I have consulted the clerics and the poets, the holy words and the wisdom of my own heart, and I have learned one thing and one thing alone: that God made us in love and wants us only to love on this earth."

I was speechless in the face of such faith and courage.

*"Eshg hich vaght gonah nist,"* he told me, and now my Farsi was fluent enough to know what he had meant and said all those months before. "I know with all my soul the truth: love is never a sin."

To hear that made me feel, for the briefest moment, that I was not a monster, that not everything I touched was evil. Because I did love. I was full of it, in the heart concealed behind my masks. I loved music and the stars and to learn and to be free and I loved the words of the poets and the smell of rain on the air and the feel of sun on my skin and the rush of lust and the thrill of magic. I loved so much, and I finally saw that, among all the wonders and horrors I had found in this distant land, I loved him most of all, and how it all was reflected in him. And I feared more than anything the loss of him.

I told him so, and it made him smile. It made him laugh like we were free. That night, he led me to the bed in that little house. He had been with other lovers, other men, in secret and in silence, and he knew what to do. We met in the darkness, and he understood my need for it. He understood all my fears. He said there was no rush, but we both knew that wasn't true.

It made my heart beat out of my chest in terror when he touched me, and I cursed his faith for denying us wine. I cursed myself that I could not let him too close, but I was not afraid of being the one to touch. So fumbling and careful, in awe and gratitude, I brought my lover what pleasure I could. Ill-suited and inept as I was, I let him do the same to me after, intoxicated by the feel of another. For the first time in months, I slept soundly for a few hours, safe and untroubled by dreams of blood.

For one day, we were allowed something like peace. We made plans of how we would escape, and we shared the sea air, and I let down my guard. I took off my mask in the sun, listened to the gulls, and let myself dream when he slipped his hand into mine. It was only in the dark, that night, that I finally allowed him to kiss me. Shrouded in shadow, I tasted his lips and how sweet they were with his laughter.

"To think the great magician could be so shy," he joked. My pride pushed me then, and I reminded him I was an eager student.

It was different than anything before. It wasn't the rush of a first fuck or the emptiness of two bodies seeking a moment of release. It was warmth and passion, seeking and finding. Caught between his thighs, I spilled and gasped as he rutted against my hips. All I wanted was to give him in return a fraction of what I felt. He laughed when I told him that, that rich, warm sound, and he said there were ways to do more, with oils and patience, and some day we could try. Some day.

In the dark that night, I had started thinking of it as real, that future with him far away from all the death and disaster I had caused. If he could love, I could hope...

Shaya found us right before sunrise. It was clear from our state, half-dressed and rumpled, what we had been doing, but Shaya chose to be blind. He didn't want to know.

"We have to go now," he told Ramin. Just Ramin. "But only us. *He* has to find his own way."

"I came this far for him, do you think I would abandon him now?" Ramin asked in return.

"Yes! He has hurt us enough!" Shaya railed. "You have destroyed your name, my name, our family's name for him, all for the sake of this *monster*! That is enough! I will not see you destroy yourself!"

"He's made his own choice," I cut in. It was one of the stupider things I ever did – trying to reason with a man hoping to save his brother's life.

"Stay out of this, demon! Can you not see how you corrupt everything you touch?" Shaya said and turned to his brother. "He is a fiend, a devil! And you do not see it! He has no soul to save."

"He does and so do you!" Ramin fought back. "He is not the root of this evil, brother! He is a victim just, like you and I. The Shah you serve – the man who would condemn you for following your conscience – he is the true criminal! He is the one who must be held to account!"

It was the worst thing he could have said with the Shah's servants waiting outside the door. They were the same deputies Shaya had enlisted to help kill me, and now, they had come to finish the job he had assigned. They shot the man who had just spoken treason first.

It happened so fast, that gunshot. That deafening, unechoing bang was the worst sound in the world. And it seemed to take forever to watch Ramin fall to the ground, red blossoming from his breast. Once again, I saw my world crumble in an instant. But this time, I was ready to take revenge, and so was Shaya. He drew his pistol, and in another instant, the man who had felled his brother had a bullet between his eyes.

The other man aimed his pistol at Shaya, but my Punjab lasso was faster and he was dead an instant after Shaya turned to see the threat. Five people had been alive in that house mere seconds before, and now, only two remained alive. In body at least. Something in both of us died as Ramin bled on the floor.

Shaya fell to his knees beside his brother's body, weeping and destroyed. I tried to speak, but he turned to me with his pistol aimed.

"Get out, fiend. You saved my life and he died for yours. Go now in honor of him and that debt before I come to my senses. Know that if I ever find you again – if I hear you have spilled blood and wasted this freedom – I will have my justice. Go and suffer, Erik. Live with this blood. You took his life with all the others. Go and live with your guilt."

I would learn years later that my destruction of Shaya's life was even more thorough than I had thought. He passed off a corpse left to the ravages of the sea as me, but he had already lost everything and betrayed the Shah. He was imprisoned for a year, then exiled, only saved from execution by the intervention of distant relations on behalf of his royal blood and the fact the Shah's will had (he thought) been done.

I fled west, numb and horrified. I traveled only at night, sometimes hiding for days and letting my grief and guilt consume me. But once again, I would not die. I couldn't. I would not throw away the life Ramin had died to save. Shaya had been right about that, and he was right that I deserved every moment of suffering and despair. I spoke to no one. I lived by theft and cunning alone. I did not wish to condemn another soul by merely being near them.

But eventually I had to return to humanity. They're all over the place, unfortunately. I joined a Roma band, buying my place among them once again with my willingness to touch all that was unclean and save them pollution and harm. I was happy to remain on the periphery as we moved west across Turkey, until I heard one of their elders playing the violin by the fire.

It was an old tune I knew, sad and full of longing, fitting for a people who had left their ancestral lands so long ago they were nothing but myth, and who were driven so often from any place that they wanted to call home. The People were home. The music and the story it told was home. And as I listened, I came home too.

The old man saw me in the shadows and offered me his instrument. It had been months since I had played and I didn't even know if I deserved to be in the presence of music, the only god I had ever worshiped, again. Was it not a sin, I thought to myself, to still feel joy or love after all that pain?

Love is never a sin, his voice whispered in my ear.

I took up the bow and touched the strings and played for love. And I came back to life. For a little while, at least.

# 7. Dies Irae

*"I'm sorry. That you lost him. That Shaya lost him too."*
*"As am I."*
*"He's with you though. He lives in your memory and in your heart."*
*"People never leave us, not really. They persist in our memory like ghosts.*
*Sometimes I'm still haunted by him. Sometimes it's others voices I hear. I*
*found another ghost when I finally came home. One who had never left*
*me."*

I drifted for a year more, through Turkey, then across the Hellespont back into Greece, and then Italy again. For the first time, I revisited places I had seen before, now with older eyes and a heavier heart. True, my heart had been heavy in my youth, but after Persia, it felt like a lead weight in my chest, pulling me downward every day. But I didn't drown. Indeed, if I am to extend my metaphor here, I was more like a fish than anything, the kind that swim all the way out to sea only to come home to mate and die, drawn by some memory.

That was as good an explanation as any for why I found myself back in France. I let myself know the countryside more this time, frightened of what I would find in Paris. I explored the villages and woods that were so much like the places I had known in my youth, places I had loved and hated. The Roma I traveled with found me to be a useful guide and an even more useful entrée into fairs and even the garden parties of the rich, where we would play and perform.

I sang to the stars I knew from my youth. I walked though fields of lavender and spring blossoms, the air itself humming at the light of summer returned. Each village with its old church, stonework walls, and charming bridges over the Seine looked more like "home" than the last. I really should not have been surprised when I found myself in the vicinity of Rouen, wandering the streets of the village I had never been allowed to visit by daylight as a child, shut away in our cottage at the edge of Yville-sur-Seine.

The house I had grown up in was there, but in ruin. The old Louis Phillipe furniture was weathered and cracked from exposure to the elements through the open windows. The coop where I had chased the chickens was so overgrown you could barely tell something had been there. Only a few notes sounded on the piano forte where I had first learned to use the keys. The corner where I would hide when Mama was in her madness was still there, full of cobwebs. There was the window she had broken with a book I was not supposed to read. There was the spot where I had kept my mask at night before she had forced me to sleep with it on. There was my window where I had looked out on this same sky and dreamed of a wide and wonderous world where I could find a place to be free.

All of it was dust and old dreams and nothing more, and I left without a tear. That little boy was dead, and the woman who had hurt him was dead too. They only lived inside me as ghosts, rising once in a while to haunt me in the dark.

There was one phantom from my past who still drew breath however, and part of me wanted to see him. I encouraged our caravan to linger near Yville for the summer, knowing we might be invited to perform at a soirée or carnival at any time.

In July, it happened. We received an invitation from the steward of the great château up on the hill to play for the nobles at their summer hunting party. I confirmed the name of the host. Yes, my father would be there. The steward asked my name, and I proudly told him. There are not many Eriks in the world. I wanted to give the monster a warning. I wanted him to know the ghost had come.

In my memory, my father was a shadow, a monster that lurked at the edges. He was ever-present, for it was his curse in my blood. He was the reason I was alive, the reason I was deformed. He was the reason my mother had lost her sanity and her soul. I wanted to see him and know if that hatefulness was as clear on his face as it was on mine or if he still wore as handsome a mask as I remembered.

I dressed like the magician I was, in my long cloak and hood. I wore red for the occasion. My hair was long and free, and I wore my eeriest mask, the one that made the light in my gold eyes shine all the brighter. The Punjab lasso was in my pocket, and my weapons and tricks were all ready. The Roma who came with me could sense this was a performance of special import and warned me to be careful. "They'll take your soul, Erik, these *gaje* who say they have the blood of kings. Don't listen to them when they offer you the moon – they can't hold it."

I took their advice, eventually, but by that point it was too late.

It was a fine party, the finest I had attended since my time at the court of the Shah, and in so many ways it reminded me of those rosy hours. The attendees were men, mainly, there to hunt in my father's lands and woods, and the women were all mistresses and courtesans. Their wives would be inconvenient. They all must have been friends, for there are so few elites they all know of one another, and my father had given invitations to barons of industry and of blood, counts and marquis. Only a few were given the honor of a room in the château for the night, it turned out.

I explored the château while we waited to go on. And, yes, by explore, I do mean I looked for things to steal. It was my inheritance, after all. I was surprised to find that the old Baroness, my grandmother, seemed to still be alive and keeping a room there, though she was absent from the festivities. This was a time for men to be men, it seemed. I found her gold ring in her old room. I took it and placed it in my pocket, next to the little flute I had found beneath my mother's old bed.

Someone saw me leaving the house, but I paid them no mind. I didn't care at all about the scoffing fools that had come to shoot foxes and solve the world's problems in a cloud of cigar smoke, except for the one I had come to judge. Or perhaps torment. I wasn't sure.

When I began to play, I didn't look to their faces, nor when I showed off my illusions. I only looked to the man in the highest seat at the center of his lovely garden. I watched as he grew paler – a hard task given the fairness of his skin and hair, and that his eyes were already like ice. He knew the name of the man he had hired. He saw my mask and heard my voice. But I don't think he really believed until the end, when I proudly and defiantly took off my mask.

I closed my eyes and savored the warmth of the sun on my face in the sight of my father.

The crowd gasped in horror, but my father was not appalled by my face. He was afraid of me for so many other reasons.

"Who are you?" my father asked, daring to draw near.

"Red Death, come to exact revenge," I laughed. My father looked as I imagine Prince Prospero did when a phantom in crimson came to bring bloody justice to his ball. They were all like the nobles of Poe's tale to me: wicked, greedy fools who celebrated and reveled while the world died and starved outside their walls. "You may call me Erik though. Like my mother did. I come for justice for her."

And at that he laughed. I cannot blame him. It is exactly what I would have done.

"I'm sure you must be mistaken, monster, since you and your vagrants are the only criminals I see. Seize these thieves!"

Once again, my arrogance and impulsivity came to bite me squarely in the ass. I had not counted on the fear and speed of the crowd, nor the guards with pistols in their hands. I had not taken into account my own unwillingness to kill at that very moment, for doing so would have damned the Roma at my side. I did not fight when they took us and dragged us into the cellars, and I called out to my compatriots in their secret tongue to run at night when the signal came.

The nobles bound my wrists and beat me, calling me a thief and a monster. My father wasn't among them. I must admit it was the most thorough thrashing I had experienced in a while. I just laughed as my ribs cracked and my skin bruised. I laughed because my father was likely stewing in fear knowing I was in his house. What did he think I wanted? Even I didn't know.

It would do nothing to kill him, and I had promised, in my way, to Shaya that I would not waste the life Ramin had saved in shedding blood. Not that Shaya would ever know, but Ramin's ghost would. Did I just want him to admit his crimes? Did I want him to acknowledge me as his son? Why did I care?

No matter, it was time to escape, and it was easy to do so, at least from my bonds. There were guards near the entrance to the cellar, up in the kitchen. But someone had left an oil lamp on the step, right near some kindling. The kitchen was empty and the stairs to the cellar were far from the sleeping guests and residents. It should have been safe. I thought it was a safe distraction to set the fire and send the guards running down, giving me enough time.

I didn't know the unseen evil that would spread that blaze. I didn't see the shadow following after me. I went to the Roma in the servants' quarters and let them out. By the time they were out of the door, the whole house was ablaze and the alarm had gone up. The house was full of screams coming from the flames.

Never before had I felt such instant horror at my own actions, such visceral shame and regret. The screaming from the bedrooms filled my mind with images of heavy curtains engulfed by flames, four poster beds ablaze. And it was because of me. I ran towards the flames, towards the stairs and up to where I could hear people calling for help.

I could save them, I believed it. I heaved one door open, and fire exploded from inside. The poor soul inside shoved past me as they rushed to safety. A beam fell. blocking my way before I could follow, and suddenly, I was trapped.

Then I heard the one voice in that house that I knew. I heard my father screaming. "My son! Please! Help me! Don't leave me! My son!"

I knew where to find him, even as the hall filled with smoke and fire. The grandest bedroom of the house, one of the beautiful places where he had done such ugly and horrible things to my mother. The room with the window where she had jumped to her death.

I forced my way in, shoving past a beam wreathed in flame and earning new scars from the fire as it engulfed me. I pushed through, my left shoulder taking the most damage, and then I was inside. And there he was, pinned under a fallen bookshelf, trapped. Just like she had been.

"Erik! Please help me!" He sounded so desperate as he choked as he writhed. "My first-born son! You are the one who deserves my fortune! My lands! I'll give it to you! All of it! Just help me!"

The monster I had hated all my life looked so pathetic among the ashes and fire as he fought for breath.

"Are you begging me? Like she begged you?" I asked calmly from above. "Do you just want it to stop? Do you want me to let you go?"

"Yes! Please!" he cried. "Please save me!"

I looked down into his face. The gold of the fire reflected in his blue eyes so finally, they looked like mine. Sad and pitiful and still monstrous. His legacy was not the gold and lands he offered me, it was the pain and suffering he had caused and finally knew. That was the legacy I would inherit and spend. He had made me this monster. They all had. They all deserved to burn.

So did I, but I would not burn with them.

I turned away and he screamed. I didn't look back as I went to the window. The fire had already exploded the glass. I stood where Sarah Gilbride had chosen to die and jumped in order to live, leaving the man who killed her to an agonizing end. I managed to catch a ledge and slow my fall. It hurt, crashing to the earth, but I lived. I kept living for the next few days out of pure hatred and spite.

I ran from the manor, the agony of my wounds and the horror at what I had done and become and what had been done once more to me finally reaching me past my shock and panic. There was still screaming and chaos as I fled into the night, barely able to move with the pain.

Even after the sound of the conflagration and the screams of people dying in the fire were gone from my ears, I heard them in my head and heart. They followed me. All the screams of pain and terror I had caused for my entire miserable life followed me as I ran. I had left the author of all that pain to die, and for what? I was their monster more than ever.

I was in more pain than I had ever been, in body and soul, and I still refused to die. I kept breathing through every minute that I thought would be the last but wasn't. I learned, as I had so many times, how much I could survive. That I *would* survive.

I broke into a barn when morning came, hiding from the burning rays of the sun like a nocturnal beast. I tended my wound with what I could steal. I had nothing on me but my lasso, my mother's little flute, and the ring I had stolen from my grandmother's room.

I slept – or tried to, as the pain and nightmares kept me awake – and didn't move until nightfall. I stole a cloak and horse and finally put as much distance as I could between myself and the smoldering ruins of the château I had made into my father's pyre.

I headed east. Somewhere in the delirium of pain and hate that had consumed me, I had decided on where I would go. I would rest there, either to heal, or for eternity. I would go to the Opera.

It took me two full nights of riding and four stolen horses to get to Paris, following the Seine. I arrived just before dawn, when I found an entrance to the catacombs at the edge of the city and slipped into the welcoming dark of the underground. It took me another day of moving through the maze of tunnels, sewers, and caves beneath Paris to find my way to the vicinity of Charles Garnier's great palace of art. It was finally close to completion. I was just in time.

Much had changed in the years since the building had been taken back from the Commune. Artisans had adorned the public spaces with mosaics, murals, and gold. Statues of nymphs held dark candelabras at the foot of the *grand escalier*, and the auditorium filled with red velvet seats was nearly complete, the huge chandelier that would soon hang high above the seats lowered down for finishing touches before installation.

Some things, however, were the same. My hollow column was still there, waiting for me in box five; as was the mirror covering our preferred secret path down to the lake, in dressing room thirteen. Triggering that entrance was a trial, not because the mechanism was hard to use, but because I had lost my mask and using that mirror meant I saw my reflection. I saw my face, something I had avoided doing for years.

There it was: the face of a corpse. Of The Living Death. I looked more terrible than even my worst memories, beaten and burnt and soiled, like I had truly been spat out of hell and dug my way out of a grave. I saw my eyes, glowing gold like fire. I saw in that mirror everything that my father had made me, that Steiner had made me, that the Shah had made me, that the nobles and oligarchs and cruel men of the world had made me.

And I was one of them, wasn't I? I had lit the flame in the forge, I had fashioned myself into this creature – the worst of the world and the worst of them. I could look away from the glass, but I knew what my reflection was: A monster. A dead, awful thing.

So I would go to where the dead belonged.

I descended into the underworld, hate and pain consuming me. Here I was in the ruins of my old dream, the dream of burning the old world to the ground and starting anew. But there was no restarting for me. Laurent had been right all those years ago. Maybe complete destruction of this monument to the bourgeois was the answer, but with them in it.

The idea made so much sense. My work was unfinished. My revenge was unfinished, and I was damned forever now. I could do anything. I would go to the tomb of my fellow communards and finally finish our work. One fire had not been enough, I swore through the madness of my pain and the fever that had claimed me. I needed to burn it *all* to the ground at last, or at least the monument where the great and powerful worshipped themselves when they should be worshipping music.

I found my way to the compartments on the side of the lake, and it felt like walking into a graveyard. There was a coldness there that went deep into my soul as I examined the walls where our prisoners had carved their initials in a last hope at being remembered before the dark consumed them. Through my fever and mania, they whispered to me, pushing me onward.

I moved on to my old room, the one that had once been a refuge. Everything was still there: my hidden store of candles and paper and ink and blankets, my (now rotten) stash of food, even a pile of moldering books waited for me. And beside all of that: the mirrors of our makeshift torture chamber and Laurent's cache of gunpowder. Everything I needed to bring death to myself and everyone above.

I saw it in my mind, the fires of hell rising through the Opera at the opening performance, like the Commendatore coming to take Don Juan down to damnation. But this time, it would be the unrepentant sinner that rose to take them, as I had always imagined, as I had always hoped. I would be Don Juan, rejected from earth and heaven and even the inferno. I would finally have my revenge on them all, as the world above had always deserved from me!

I should have eaten or slept, but my burns and wounds had festered, and the fever had its claws deep in me. Or maybe it was just some rot in my soul or the ghosts of that place seizing on my weakened state. I didn't rest. I started composing. I composed and I planned. I wrote in ink the color of blood, scrawling music and hideous dreams of destruction into the score that burst from my mind. I kept going until I collapsed, Laurent's voice in my head, telling me to stay alive and wait for the right time. Soon it would come.

I woke in the dark, but it was not complete darkness. There was a silver tinge to it, a whisper in the air that reminded me of the night in the Cave of Cats or that monastery in Warsaw. It was a ghostly light, and I knew I was not alone. I wondered if I was one of the ghosts now too. I think I was close. But I heard a whisper through all the noise compelling me to kill and destroy and share all my pain.

*You are more than an executioner.*

When I awoke again, the fever had broken. I looked at the mess around me, carnage written in notes and diagrams. I had lived in a nightmare of rage and hate and destruction for days and now I was awake. I needed to wait, I told myself. I needed to prepare and live until it was time. For now, I could put it down. Couldn't I? Or should I give it up?

I needed to live first and I was still on the edge of that. I made my way back up to the theater, weak, exhausted, and still in pain. I needed food and clothes, which I found easily. The Opera was more alive than it had been during the war – full of workers bestowing finishing touches. But as I was eating my stolen bread so fast that I nearly choked, I realized it was not just workers. The musicians had come too.

It was Bach that I first heard wafting through the halls. The first cello sonata. A member of the orchestra had come early; to practice, perhaps. It was perfect and beautiful and for those precious moments while I listened to those notes, all my pain and hate and rage melted away. How could I have forgotten how much beauty there could be in a few notes? How could I contemplate destroying someone who crafted such melodies? I returned to my refuge in shame and hid the unfinished score away.

It didn't last long, that first bout of conscience.

A few days later, as I stole a new mask and clothes, someone saw me in the shadows before I could put the mask on and they screamed. In a fit of hate, I spent the days after rebuilding the torture chamber... Until I saw myself again in the glass and fled my crimes and hatefulness in fear again.

I built walls after that, to hide the chamber away. The gun powder I hid too, beneath the floors. And then I kept building, dividing my new flat into tidy rooms. I kept going up to listen to the new opera company that had begun to practice and rehearse, even though the building was not entirely done. The old Opera on the *Rue Le Peletier* had burned down years before, and all of those who had survived were grateful for the grand new building to make their own.

They had survived one fire – how terrible it would be to give them another. And what had that fire done or changed? Nothing. But maybe, the horrible voice in my head said, maybe it had just not been big enough. That was what the whispers said, and I wanted to tell them no.

For the next few months, I was a battlefield, two sides of me vying for control. I was Scheherazade, telling myself a new tale every night to keep myself and those above alive, to give myself a reason to stay. And there were so many reasons. I kept building, giving myself new challenges and tasks. A fireplace, a washroom. Bright lights for my room of horrors too.

I went back and forth, composing my terrible *Don Juan Triumphant* one day, and turning to calmer music to soothe myself the next. My house on the lake – and it was a house – had started to fill with instruments and furniture I borrowed from the world above.

Books too. So many books. And tools and little bits of beauty and wonder. I could easily travel all through the city when I wanted, even into the cellars of the Louvre itself.

I thrived on distractions and new obsessions, as I always had. In the winter, I found Cecilia. That was the name the pipe organ in the old, destroyed church had been given before I rescued her. It was another great distraction, to move her piece by piece in the night and rebuild her in my own home.

That was what I had, all of a sudden. As 1874 drew to a close, I looked around and found myself in the home I had dreamed of for years. It was perfect. Everything I wanted, safe under the ground. There was no one down there to scream at my face, no reflections but the ones I brought myself. And I could avoid looking at those. And there was music. Endless music. I could make my own or take in all I wanted. In fact, I was becoming quite invested in the company above as they prepared for the grand opening of the Palais Garnier.

They, in turn, had become quite interested in me, I discovered.

I had tried to be careful running my little errands in the building above. I used my secret passages and trap doors, but there were only so many and I am not a small person. I had been seen many times after the first encounter with the firefighter who saw my face. And the fact that things kept disappearing drew suspicion too. A few days before the opening of the Opera, I was behind a curtain as the dancers were leaving the stage and heard a baller rat whisper to her friend: "Don't go that way! The other day Yvette saw the Phantom in that hall."

Every good theater has at least one ghost (and in my time in the cellars, I had confirmed that the Opera had more than her share). Any place where things move in the dark – like firefighters and ratcatchers – will breed legends. But thanks to me, the Opera had a highly active specter in residence, and there were more stories every day among the company about the Opera Ghost. It was not a career I had meant to take on, but just like the home I had found, it was perfect. Almost like destiny.

The management received their first correspondence from the Ghost soon after the grand opening of the theater. I had watched the gala performance of *La Juive* from the flies and it had been a middling experience in terms of acoustics. I wanted a box, and thanks to the hollow column that remained from my work years before, I knew exactly which one would be mine. Box five on the grand tier was to be reserved for the Phantom if the Opera wished to avoid bad luck. It was a simple request, and it only took me giving a few patrons the fright of their lives for me to assure it was honored.

I was sitting in my box, bored with another pompous overture from Meyerbeer and thinking how the Opera was not living up to her full potential, when I realized I no longer had any desire to destroy the place. I would not doom the hundreds of workers and artists that inhabited the Opera to death along with the bourgeois in the audience. This was my home, and I had no desire but to enjoy it now that I had found it.

I returned to my *Don Juan* periodically in the months after, the hellish music I had composed for my first and final public triumph still seething out of my injured soul, but the fire behind it had died down into embers. There was still a spark, of course, but I hid away the trigger to the gun power. I made the trigger into a Grasshopper, and then shut it away in its casket. And I also made a Scorpion, a trigger to flood the gun powder with water, ready for when, perhaps, I wouldn't need or want the means to blow a hole in Paris. They were both there, waiting.

They waited for years. They waited as I found new diversions and fixations. I filled my home with instruments, curiosities, borrowed art from the Louvre's cellars, books in every language, and reams of newer, kinder compositions. I still filled my music with my sorrow, with my loneliness and grief, but in the dark I was finally safe from all the pain.

Once again, I was at peace when I was with the music, bodyless and free. An insubstantial shadow. A phantom.

Maybe I *had* died, I thought often. Maybe that night when *Don Juan* had first seized my soul, I hadn't woken up. Maybe I was a real ghost too. There were some days when I truly could not tell, and many others where I decided it did not matter. I was *Le Fantôme de l'Opéra*, hidden deep in the shadows. I was a being of magic and darkness, a cursed thing, The Living Death. All that I had always been since birth and more. I was a legend and, in my way, I was content.

The reminder that I did not deserve contentment came after three years. I saw him in the audience from my box, high in the cheapest seats. Even without his Astrakhan cap, I would have known Shaya Motlagh anywhere. I wondered if the poor souls who encountered the Phantom in the halls of the Opera felt as I did when I saw the Daroga, as if the past and death itself were reaching out to pull them back.

I thought it might have been a coincidence, but then he came to the next performance. And the next. He began to haunt the streets around the Opera. I knew because I watched him. Then he came inside, looking for something. So I saved him time. I appeared behind him as he was examining a mural in the grand salon and greeted him.

"Good evening, Daroga."

You can imagine the way he jumped at my voice. I think you also can imagine the hate in his eyes when he turned to me. You've seen it yourself, sadly. What ensued can't quite be termed a conversation. Rather, he told me with all the spite and vitriol I deserved of what had befallen him after I had escaped Persia. How dare I live free when he had suffered so long and been driven from his home?

He had searched for me, a task which was not easy, but he knew me better than anyone; my secrets and the places I would go. He had guessed Paris correctly and spent months searching the fairs and freakshows near the city for signs of me, until he heard a rumor that the new opera house was haunted by a specter in a mask.

"And now I find you. Not a magician, but a goddamn ghost." I remember the way he said it, as if a ghost was the worst insult possible. "I should have killed you."

"Doesn't it make you happy to know I'm stuck in limbo, just like you?" I asked back.

"I'll be happy when you're the one in exile or in prison," he replied. "I'll find a way to put you there. I swear it."

"Good luck then," I said before I disappeared from sight.

I was worried, at first – terrified actually – that Shaya would destroy everything I had built. My heart seized every time I imagined him exposing me and sending me to another cage. I spent several nights in sleepless terror, afraid of what he might take from me. But the blow never fell, and I realized that the only reason I was so afraid was because of how much haunting the Opera had come to mean to me. Shaya for his part was a smart man (not as smart as me, but intelligent enough), and he knew I was too well-protected behind my Opera's walls. So he waited. He watched. And I went on.

Maybe he was satisfied with my punishment, as he saw it. After all, some part of him wanted me dead and I was. I had died in the cottage by the Caspian, and I had died again in the fires of my father's manor. I had died so many times before then: when I was a child who had never known innocence, and a freak of nature who yearned to be free. I died in Venice when I learned the ways of the flesh and how even my touch was a curse, and in India when I became a killer without remorse.

That is the way of things, I had learned, living and dying. We become new people, don news masks with every changing year and season. And then, we let them go and become someone else, like the earth herself, always born again. Real death, I thought, meant the end of that cycle – no more chances to start anew or see a new reflection of yourself in another's eyes.

In that way, I was finally, truly a phantom, for I never intended to let another person truly see me again. I was The Living Death made real

– haunting a temple to the music I loved, with my own music and voice to never be heard. For six years, I remained dead. I learned and I hid and I stopped believing I would ever change.

Until I took César for a ride one October morning, and returned him late to the stables. And fate placed a miracle in my path. Fate sent me you.

You know the story from there.

I never really chose the melodies of my symphony, the different things I have become. They seem to have chosen me. Monstrous child, wandering magician, communard and torturer, architect and executioner. Phantom. And then... Angel.

If I could choose to be one thing again, looking back, it would be that. Even knowing the pain and the heartbreak that came when I fell, I would choose to be an Angel of Music again. I had found everything in the world I thought I deserved, perhaps even more. Then to give hope to a woman who made the world brighter with her kindness, I reached out to the light. For her, I would give up the home I had built. For her, I would give up everything.

For you. To be the man I see reflected in your eyes, to be worthy of your light, I would endure any darkness.

*"That is a rather strange way to end things."*

*"Because the symphony is unfinished, for now."*

*"I'm happy to know there is another movement to be written. Or more."*

*"Another beginning on a distant shore, born anew with the sunrise."*

# Acknowledgements

Thank you to the friends and family who have constantly supported me, especially when I said I wanted to write a whole extra novella in the midst of writing another novel. Special thanks to Ana, Jordan, Lisa, Ruby and Saba for helping to make this book the best it could be.

To my wife, for talking me through plot problems, listening to me rave about history and still being willing to read the finished product, I love you. Thank you to to my mom, for reading and editing for me and pretending she didn't see the sexy parts. To Marlon, for furry therapy and reminding me when it's time to take a break for walkies. And to Tam, for giving me a reason to keep going on the hardest days.

# Don't miss out!

Visit the website below and you can sign up to receive emails whenever Jessica Mason publishes a new book. There's no charge and no obligation.

https://books2read.com/r/B-A-RZHV-TZIOC

**BOOKS 2 READ**

Connecting independent readers to independent writers.

Did you love *Erik's Tale*? Then you should read *Angel's Mask*[1] by Jessica Mason!

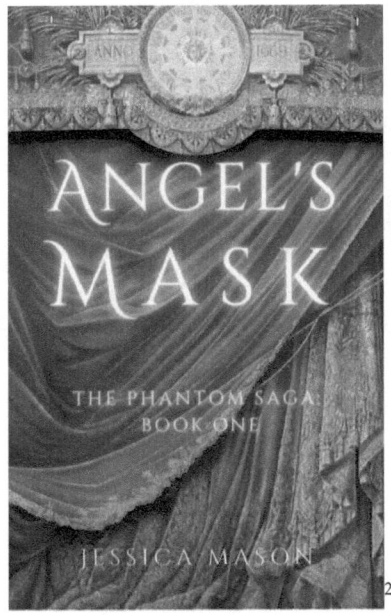[2]

The timeless tale of The Phantom of the Opera brought to life as never before...

Christine Daaé arrives penniless and hopeless at the steps of the great Paris Opera House, in search of an angel. What finds her instead is a man in a mask named Erik, a tortured soul masquerading as a ghost. Fascinated by Christine, Erik dons a new mask to be close to her: that of the Angel of Music.

This strange patron awakens Christine's voice and soul...as well as desires she cannot understand. Their adoration growing, Erik and Christine remain separated by deception and darkness, tangled in a web of lust and lies. How far will Erik go to be close to his eager

1. https://books2read.com/u/3LVdjJ

2. https://books2read.com/u/3LVdjJ

student? And will Christine be able to forgive her angel, when she finally sees past his mask to the monster beneath?

The first novel in *The Phantom Saga* takes readers on a lush, erotic journey from the depths of Paris's catacombs to the glittering, ruthless world of the Opera's stage. Full of diverse characters, rich detail, and intoxicating romance, *Angel's Mask* reinvents the legend of the Phantom and Christine with passion and twists that will leave readers breathless.

# Also by Jessica Mason

**The Phantom Saga**
Angel's Mask
Angel's Kiss
Erik's Tale

# About the Author

Jessica Mason lives near Portland, Oregon with her wife, daughter, and corgi. She has studied opera, practiced law, and has worked as a fandom journalist and podcaster, among many varied careers. But first and foremost she has always been a storyteller. When she manages to stop writing, she enjoys gardening, travel, music, and witchcraft.

Find her on social media: @ByJessicaMason

## About the Publisher

Murmuration Books is an independent publisher bringing readers, steamy, spellbinding, spooky, sensational stories. We are committed to diverse themes, new authors, and creative takes on old ideas.

For more, visit Murmurationbooks.com

www.ingramcontent.com/pod-product-compliance
Lightning Source LLC
Chambersburg PA
CBHW022031170626
46808CB00003B/1150